STRING OF PEARLS

Tony Ayres is a screenwriter. Currently, he is writing his first collection of short stories, a miniseries for the ABC and developing a documentary about men's sexual fantasies entitled 'Ten Inch Tongue'. 'My Cock lives in Hell' is his second published short story and *String of Pearls* his first work as an editor.

STRING OF PEARLS

Stories about cross-dressing

EDITED BY TONY AYRES

ALLEN & UNWIN

'Elegy' by John A. Scott has been previously published in John A. Scott's, *Selected Poems*, UQP, Brisbane, 1995.

Publication of this title was assisted by The Australia Council, the Federal Government's arts funding and advisory body.

Australia Council for the Arts

First published in 1996 by
Allen & Unwin Pty Ltd
9 Atchison Street, St Leonards, NSW 2065 Australia

National Library of Australia
Cataloguing-in-Publication entry:

String of Pearls: stories about cross-dressing.

ISBN 1 86373 914 9.

1. Transvestites—Fiction. 2. Short stories, Australian.
I. Ayres, Tony.

A823.0108355

Set in 11/13 Amerigo by DOCUPRO, Sydney
Printed by Australia Print Group, Maryborough, Victoria

10 9 8 7 6 5 4 3 2 1

To Michael

CONTENTS

CONTRIBUTORS

Paul Allatson lives in Sydney and writes on Sundays. He is currently amassing a collection of very short stories. There is only one bird—Oscar, vivacious and blue—in his aviary.

Tony Ayres is a screenwriter. Currently, he is writing his first collection of short stories, a miniseries for the ABC and a documentary about men's sexual fantasies called 'Ten Inch Tongue'. *String of Pearls* is his first work as an editor.

Belinda Chayko grew up on the north coast of New South Wales. She was a journalist with the *Sydney Morning Herald* before turning to film and now works as a writer–director. Her short films have been successful at Australian and international festivals, and her work has been screened on ABC and SBS-TV.

Gary Dunne lives in Sydney. His published fiction includes *If Blood Should Stain the Lino* (1983) and *As If Overnight* (1990).

His 1993 novel *Shadows on the Dance Floor* is now being adapted for the screen. He has also edited several anthologies of gay and lesbian writing, most recently *FRUIT* (1994).

Nick Enright is a Sydney playwright whose work for the theatre includes *Daylight Saving, Mongrels, Good Works* and *Blackrock*, and the books and lyrics for several musicals. He has also written for radio, film and television. This is his first published fiction.

Catherine Lazaroo was born in Western Australia and has been involved in devising and writing for theatre from an early age. After eight years of juggling writing with a career in medicine, she is now pursuing her writing full-time. Travels include a stint at a TB hospital in rural Pakistan. She lives with a red-cloud kelpie.

Fiona McGregor was born in Sydney and has lived there most of her life. She is the author of a novel, *Au Pair* (1993), and a book of interlinked short stories, *Suck My Toes* (1994), which won the Steele Rudd Award.

Gillian Mears lives near Grafton, New South Wales. She has written four books, most recently *The Grass Sister* (1995).

Louis Nowra was born in Melbourne and lives in Sydney. He is the author of such plays as *Inner Voices, Visions, Inside the Island, The Golden Age, Radiance, Cosi, Summer of the Aliens* and *The Incorruptible*. He wrote the screenplays *Map Of The*

Human Heart and *Cosi*. His novels are *The Misery of Beauty* and *Palu*.

Dorothy Porter is a poet, writer of adolescent fiction and song writer. Her eighth book, *The Monkey's Mask*, a lesbian detective romance novel in verse, won the *Age* Poetry Book of the Year in 1994 and was joint winner of the National Book Council's Turnbull Fox Phillips Poetry Prize in 1995. A new book of verse, *Crete*, will be published by Hyland House in 1996.

John A. Scott was born in England in 1948. Author of twelve books of poetry and prose, he has received a number of major Australian writing awards, including Victorian Premier's Prizes for his book of poetic narratives, *St Clair*, and for his novel, *What I Have Written*. A new sequence of short novels, *Passages*, will be published by Penguin Books in 1996.

Chad Taylor lives in Auckland where he writes fiction and screenplays. He has written two novels, *Pack of Lies* and *Heaven*, and a collection of short stories, *The Man Who Wasn't Feeling Himself*.

Alana Valentine is the recipient of a NSW State Literary Award, a Churchill Fellowship, and the 1994 ANPC/New Dramatists Award. Alana has written for stage, film and radio, and her essays and stories have been published in various newspapers and magazines. Her first anthologised short story was published in 1995 in *Divertika*.

William Yang is best known as a photographer of the
Sydney social scene. He has combined writing with photo-
graphy in his books *Starting Again* and *Patrick White*, and
further combined the two with performance in his mono-
logues with slide projections. *Sadness*, the most successful
of these, has toured extensively in Australia and overseas.

HER AVIARY

PAUL ALLATSON

I

The inspector has asked me for a description of her. He has been kind, surprisingly so, gentle and soft voiced, and everything I need has been supplied. I have ample paper and a box of pens, coffee, an assortment of biscuits, a jug of water, an ashtray. The inspector is in no hurry, I can take all the time in the world, which is just as well since I have watched the minute hand's crawl from twelve to six and back again without disturbing the ream of solid whiteness in front of me.

I assume that I am required to begin with her face. After all, that is why I have been chosen to do this, over my brother and my two sisters, over my father, broken, whimpering, his memory failing him under the weight of all this uncertainty, his eyes useless for the last three days, the period of her absence. I am my mother's son people have always told me, as they go to great pains to tell me now. Photographs would prove it if they could be found. There used to be boxes of them, hundreds of her, but they have vanished, a mystery the inspector regards as significant—that none of us can show him a photograph of our own mother, that Dad cannot locate a single image of his wife of forty years.

3

So I should begin by writing about her face, echo to mine, as if my face, our shared features, provide me with a privileged position from which to define her. But what is the point? What does it matter that my overbite, my hazel eyes, my long, angled face so obviously derive from her? I have thought about this for well over an hour, which is why, rather than concentrate solely on her face, I am about to pick up my pen and the first piece of paper and write about how . . .

II

. . . they begin on her neck, an important point because the face has survived unscathed, the face of a 60-year-old woman weathered by an average life's addiction to sun, a face criss-crossed by fine grooves, especially where years of smoking pouts have left indentations around the lips. The face is handsome but unremarkable when compared to the rest of her. It is at the neck that the first thin line of pink is noticeable, flowing from near the left ear lobe to where it reaches whatever collar she has on and disappears from view. A neat, unambiguous scar.

I will dispense with the collar and other items of clothing because, of course, her skin can reveal nothing until it is exposed to other eyes. The first thing that would strike someone with no knowledge of her would be the skin seemingly held in place by the healed joins of wounds. Her skin has been so tanned that the pale scars stand out as if in relief, recalling the spontaneous gestures on canvas of some drug-driven artist. It would be an error to retain this conviction, however haphazard the markings, for apart from those left by the car crash—the ancient ones lying almost invisible under later arrivals—the majority did not result from accident but from the hands of surgeons. Look closely and you will see, some distance from the lines but parallel to them on both sides, the points of entry for needle and thread.

It may be difficult for a stranger to believe that surgeons were responsible for the slashes on my mother's surface. It may be difficult to imagine what medical purpose inspired some of the cuts, what diseased bits of the interior needed such generous openings before they could be attended to. The scars splay from ear to groin, beneath her breasts and over stomach, down the length of the spine, along arms and legs, the top of the right foot, the palm of the left hand. Study them and the scars begin to communicate, haptic marks that reveal the moods and skilfulness, or lack thereof, of the surgeons. An observant person would have no trouble identifying the handiwork of twelve men, for they were all men, these professional cutters.

An observant person might even recognise that the marks of the twelve reveal an inescapable fact of life: that two, perhaps three, really knew what they were doing, six were just doing a job, their minds at times elsewhere, their inattentions forever recorded by a slip of scalpel here, a sloppy stitch mark there, and three, perhaps four, of them had no idea at all, littering the skin with their false openings, slicing horizontally when they should have been aiming for a vertical, tearing instead of cutting, gouging, filleting and closing again, as if the body beneath them, at the time thankfully unable to groan in protest at their inept touch, was not a body at all but an approximation of human form, perhaps housed in a soft plastic that could never bruise, perhaps made three dimensional by the insertion of false organs manufactured to mimic the work of human ones, as if the blood was mere coloured water pumped into a thing that, despite arms and legs and a head, had never

5

lived, and would, therefore, be unlikely to suffer from the onslaught, as if the slightly parted lips could never articulate discomfort, as if the ability to walk steadily in the future was an idle and ridiculous consideration, as if the tears that would ooze from this mannequin's eyes on seeing the damage done would result from a trick of light and could therefore be of no consequence during an operation to remove the fetid or repair the malfunctioning.

Picture that skin, I will tell the inspector . . .

III

. . . and you will begin to see my mother.

– Yes, well, this is not . . . quite what I was expecting. Now, don't get me wrong, it's important to know she has scars, but we actually require something a little more . . . substantial. Specifics that I can put in the bulletin, information to go with a face, you know, that will help if we need to identify a . . . Look, I'll give you half an hour more. I've arranged for the police artist to come in around 11. It's really quite straightforward. We'll use identikits and your verbal description and we should be able to get something to go on.

– OK. What's the time now?

– It's half past ten.

IV

. . . in the morning and it seems to me that it has always been half past ten in the morning. From the desk I can see outside, a glimpse of grey sky and darker grey walls. The window is open to allow a breeze to enter, an unsatisfactory attempt to relieve the humidity. My neck and back are sticky with sweat because the weather has, in under twelve hours, changed from yesterday's pleasant and unseasonal coolness into summer with a vengeance. The breeze brings with it a stench of sweetness from the beer factory three streets away, and from somewhere in the distance, a whiff or smoke, a hint of plastic melting. Along the windowsill the bogongs are covered with dust. It is impossible to tell if they are hibernating or whether they have indeed perished, their migration thwarted by the glass rising above them.

I am supposed to be continuing my description but it is 10.40 in the morning and it has always been 10.40 in the morning. The coffee has gone steamless in the cup, and as I doodle on the paper I notice how ink has stained the surface of the fingers holding the pen. I look down at the paper and begin to write the alphabet, a little trick my mother once told me about, an option for those occasions dominated by distractions rather than application to the task at hand.

A to Z. Write down the alphabet when you are at an impasse, elaborate on it, and you will break the hold of indecision. A to Z. And as I think about it certain words come to mind, words that seem to belong to her, that have dogged her for years, her words, her voice, her life, her aviary (her haven, her love), her afternoons of boredom spent treading the slow path between laundry and clothes-line, her calamities, which none of us ever took seriously, at times seeing in them proof of an inaptitude for mother-hood, her determination, despite her bowing back, the emigration, her escape to this, a promised place that seemed to fail her expectations, her family, her garrulous-ness, her brandy-assisted voicing of her disaffections and aspirations, the hearth before which she tried to warm her ice-bound limbs, the sighs of her if onlys, her recollections of all that she could have done, her jocularity, her desperate laughter when attached to plastic bags dripping plasma, her kitchen, her prison, her loyalty, her love so constantly tested, her mouth from which she would remove her false front teeth to ease the effort of chewing, her nerves, strained, shot, but never in public, her organisation that kept us away from the circuit of chaos, her perfume, another country's scent, lily of the valley, her quivering lips whenever one of us scratched at her opinions with disparaging commentary, her resolve that someday this would all be over, her sadness, the sobs stifled by her pillow in the early morning hours, her tenderness whenever any of us required our mother's touch, her ubiquity, taken as an eternal given by a family that could not have imagined life without her, her vehemence that one day there would be no more sacrifices, her walk, lop-sided, the drag of the right leg, shortened by a few centimetres after her fifth operation, the drawer full of her x-rays, a catalogue of the disintegration of her insides, her conviction that in some as yet undiscovered space her youth was waiting for her to resume when ready, her despite everything zip.

It is not what the inspector is expecting but it won't harm him to read it, to carry with him on a small slip of paper, Mum's . . .

V

. . . alphabet, you've given me an alphabet of your mother? The inspector is looking exasperated. So I explain that it seemed to just come out when I started thinking about her, this whole thing has thrown me, I warned you before I started that it would be difficult for me, I don't know why you can't speak to the others, and *he* reminds me that they have not been helpful, I seem to be the only one who knows how to string a few words together, who *wants* to talk about her, and he is telling me that all Dad can do is repeat 'Why?' or 'How Could This Happen To Me?' and I say, I guess, and I shrug. He is staring at me, an expression I can't decipher. He says, they all advised me to speak to you, and I say, they would, I suppose it's because they've always thought of me as the favourite, the spoiled one, the one who Mum always confided in, and now he's leaning forward, looking straight into my eyes and asking, and did she? And I am looking right back into his eyes, they're grey, they don't blink, I would have told you if she had, and besides, they were the last ones to see her, at Sunday lunch, and he is leaning back now, into his chair, slowly blowing air out of his mouth, and he tells me, the problem I have is if they do know anything they're not letting on, they seem to have closed ranks, and I think, tell me about it, but I don't say that, I smile and suggest that they can't cope with the fact that she may have walked out on them, and now he is looking very interested, he's leaning towards me again, and he is asking me, so you think she walked out?, and I smile again because he's not giving anything away, this man, the inspector in his uniform, and I am shaking my head and saying, I don't know. To be honest, I would never have imagined she was capable of it, but it's easier to think that than other, more final possibilities, I don't know what to think or make of anything, I'm sorry, and now he is wondering how she seemed to me the last time I saw her, and I am thinking back to Saturday. I always go around on Saturdays to help her with the birds, cleaning the aviary, scraping the droppings off the perches, checking the nesting boxes, and I think about how I've been doing that for years, since I left home, and now she's gone, and I tell him it was Saturday, and mention the birds, and he asks me if she seemed agitated or preoccupied, and I say, no. Well. No. Although she was worried about the rosellas, they were sick, puffed up, shivering, and she asked me to catch them so we could give them the medicine she'd bought, but no, apart from that, it was just like any Saturday, we talked about the birds and sat for a while looking at them, she was fine. I'm sure of it. But, I think, maybe she wasn't, how could I have failed to pick that up?, and the inspector says, if she does contact you, we'll need to know, and I say, of course, I hope she . . . it would make me . . . it would be a relief, and the inspector smiles, and softly he tells me not to worry, the important thing is to find her, that's all I'm interested in at the moment, and now he's looking at his watch, time for the drawing session, are you up to it?, and I nod, of course I'm up to it, though I don't tell him how relieved I am to be distracted, from all of this questioning, from him, from thinking about her, from her, but I do say that I'm just a little pessimistic about it, you know, that the police artist, however skilled she may be, will be able to produce an image of *my* mother, a woman . . .

VI

. . . in her prime, exactly as she must have been at the beginning of the 1960s. And the wrinkles aren't right. It looks nothing like the woman you're searching for.
– Shall we try once more?
– I'm sorry inspector, but what's the point? Everything about the drawing is wrong, even her colouring. She has this beautiful tan, all over, admittedly marred by the scars you know about. But there's no sense of that here. And as for her hair, I've already told you that I couldn't even guess what her real hair would be like now. To be honest, I don't

think I have ever seen her without one of her wigs. She had over thirty of them. Everyone who knew her commented on how different her appearance was day after day, that in any given year, if she wanted to, she could take on the guise of three hundred and sixty-five different women. —That's very interesting, don't you think? It's almost as if she deliberately spent the last thirty years sowing confusion in preparation for this disappearance.

—Well, I don't know about that inspector. She just liked to dress up. She's been doing it for as long as I remember. Maybe she thought that it would make things easier, especially during those periods when she felt like an object, prodded and tugged at by doctors. Maybe it's like when you're a child and you put on a costume and you actually believe you have changed. You forget who and what and where you are . . .

—In a police station, helping me with my inquiries. I think we'll call it a morning, but if you don't mind, I'd like to see you here tomorrow morning with our artist so we can have another try at getting a decent likeness. At 8.30, if that's not too . . .

VII

. . . early for me. I am wide awake at five a.m., my left arm blazing and inflamed from the night's onslaught of mosquitoes, and I am aware that I have been dreaming, that I have been filled by a dream about her, and I am going to write this one down, if only to see it in words, to try and make some sense of it. I don't know if I will show it to the inspector because . . .

VIII

. . . today I am on a guided tour of mothers. They are arranged like statues on plinths that edge this white-stoned path that meanders into a distance of rolling hills. There is a guide. He is wearing a peaked cap, a royal blue uniform with brass buttons and gleaming black shoes. He holds a large stopwatch in his left hand. He will, he says, give no more and no less than one minute to each mother. I am supposed to be taking notes and making observations about other mothers that will be of assistance in the search for my own. So I concentrate and fill up my notebook and when I reach the last page and stop to wipe the perspiration from my brow, I hear clapping and turn to see my mother walking towards me, smiling at me, complimenting me on my persistence. I run towards her, so happy that my feet do not connect with the earth, my arms outstretched, like hers, like the wings of the birds passing overhead, and at our joyful collision the universe fills with laughter and I sink into her, my cheek supported in her ampleness, my fingers caressing the soft and pliant skin of her face and arms, as her scent fills me and I surrender myself to her, into that most familiar and comforting of positions, a mother's embrace, and I could die in peace right there, knowing that I am a part of her, a separate part yes, but connected, that I am of her and that she is with me, even when absent, that we are for each other, that I am her and she is me, that all the complexities outside us mean nothing when compared to this rightfulness, this peace. My lips touch her neck, grazing lightly over the beginning of a raised line that disappears under her collar. I touch it with my tongue and I can feel the raised bumps through which twine had once been pulled. I want to explore and discover the secrets of this line and begin to use my teeth until I feel the skin around the scar palpitate and blood gushes on to my tongue and the flesh opens like a sea commanded to part, and my chin and mouth and the tip of my nose sink into dark, unfamiliar territory. And as the tear widens, I decide that the time is right for a complete submersion into this damp cave and, to the sounds of my mother's groans, I dive into her until I can no longer see, I can no longer feel or smell anything, I can no longer breathe, it is as though I am writhing in silt, as if I am lost in it, silt that sticks to me like a shroud, silt that fills the hollow I am now clawing my way through. I am desperate to escape from this space, it is as if someone has covered my head with a sodden handkerchief, but I can't escape, I've been paralysed, I am gasping for breath, and my eyes are opening but not recognizing anything, and I know I have no option but to stay here for a while, for a few hours, for a day, by . . .

IX

. . . myself. To think. and there are a couple of things I have to do, like go around to the house today, her house, Dad's house, which I'm not looking forward to, but Dad left a message that the rosellas have died, and he wants me to collect the rest.

   — I see.

   — My problem is I've only got two cages big enough for three, maybe four budgies each, and there are eighteen birds in her aviary. I'm going to have to put them on the upstairs balcony because it's covered in. There's no back yard to speak of, plus all the neighbourhood cats congregate down there anyway. It wouldn't be safe. The landlord is not going to be happy about any of this. He's a strictly no pets man. But I have to take care of them. They're Mum's. They meant everything to her. Anyway, I can't make it today. Can I see you tomorrow? I'm going to be busy in the morning, but if it's OK I'll come in after lunch, and then I'll . . .

X

. . . probably need a couple of vodkas to go through with this, and Margaret says, look, once I'm finished nobody will recognise you, so what's your problem?, and I say yes, you're probably right, but this is all so strange, I mean, I'm going to have to take a taxi, and to be honest, I'm not sure I'll be able to go out in public, and she grins and says, keep still until the nails are dry, and she laughs at my expression and says, time for the face, and she is cleaning my skin, massaging, wiping, and I have to admit it's a nice feeling, weird, but I'm beginning to relax, and she is making my skin darker when the thought comes to me, and I jump to my feet and say, the voice!, her accent!, after all these years she's still got a strong English accent, how could I have overlooked that?, and Margaret says it's not important, it's not the voice they're looking for, and I say, yes, you're right, even though I am thinking the opposite, that the accent *is* important, after all, I'm going to all this trouble I may as well try and convince myself, at least, but I don't say this to Margaret, there are some things you don't mention, even to close friends, just in case they think yes, he's finally lost the plot, so I sit down again, and Margaret starts on the wrinkles, she's really methodical, she's aging me as I sit, and now she's doing the little indentations around the lips, and Margaret asks me what I'm going to do now, with the landlord, and she nods over at the balcony at the constant movement, and for a moment we listen to the chattering of parrots, and I tell her I've looked at a garden flat, I've got a day to decide, it's around the corner, there's enough room for the aviary, her aviary, dad doesn't want anything left that will remind him of her, and Margaret asks, what about the rent?, and I say ten dollars a week more, and she says, if it has a garden you'd be mad to pass it up, and she smiles, you'll be fine, and she asks, are you ready for the wig?, yes, now for the wig I nod, and after she positions it, and after she stands back with her hands on her hips, just looking at me, I say, excuse me, I have to go to the bathroom, because I have to see what I look like in the full-length mirror, I have to be alone with her, and when I see her I think, so that's it, that's her, I've seen her, I've seen you, and I walk slowly back to the kitchen and Margaret says, I've still got a few little touch-ups to do, and I keep standing, not really listening, because I feel as if I have no substance at all, it's like I had never quite grasped how emptying it could be to get up every single day of your life and force yourself to appear . . . untroubled . . . to convince everybody that this was you, the real you, when there was nothing inside, nothing but tiredness, a space that you could never acknowledge, because all you needed to simply persist would be to take everybody in, to stop them from penetrating the exterior, as if that was enough, as if that is all it takes to fill the days from birth to death, a body made up to distract, just like the bodies flashing around my covered-in balcony, my temporary aviary, I am thinking, I am nothing but an exhausted distraction, until Margaret shouts, for God's sake will you sit . . .

XI

. . . down.
  – I'm sorry I'm late.

– It's not a problem. I certainly wasn't expecting this.

– I hope you don't mind, but I've given it a lot of thought. I just couldn't bear another session like the other day, you know: 'No, not like that, the eyebrows were a little thicker, and no, you haven't understood about the wrinkles around the mouth.' This way you at least get the substantial image you've been asking me for.

– Well, I suppose . . .

– I know what you're thinking, inspector. But really, even though I couldn't find any of Mum's wigs and I had to promise the moon to be able to borrow this one from my next door neighbour, and I'm not sure if she would have worn one quite like this, this *is* a pretty good likeness, as good as you're going to get.

– Look, I have to be honest with you. I've never encountered anything like this in my whole . . .

– Inspector, why don't you go and ask the photographer to come in before I have second thoughts? Trust me, the photographs will prove it. Show them to Dad and the others and you'll realise you've got the image of the woman you're looking for. They'll be screaming at you to tell them where she is. Now I would love to picture that, only . . .

XII

. . . one more to go, a frontal shot. So I turn to face him, and as I do I bring my left hand up to the base of my neck and I scratch, slowly, there, where the itch is, and when the photographer asks me to turn a little more to the right, to lift my chin, stop, fine, I move my index finger up and behind the lobe to where the line begins, and my finger slides down to where it disappears under my collar, and I steel myself in anticipation of the request to smile.

INSTRUCTIONS TO MY SEAMSTRESS

CATHERINE LAZAROO

I have sent for you today, Madame Picot, because I have some more work for you. See these lengths of cloth? Five yards of satin, raven black, seven yards of fine silk crêpe in a dark-wood green and dotted with the white flowers of hemlock, and some chantilly lace besides for trim, which I myself have dyed the exact shade of ash. I entrust them to you who have fashioned the most apt and telling of my costumes, and I beg you, by the craft of your hand and the art of your eye, to make of them a gown in which I would be glad to die.

Is that the purpose of this gown? You look at me with horror and you shake your head. Do you refuse? I will pay you well, name your own price, two hundred, three hundred guineas, more. Listen to me. We will strike a bargain.

This is what I need from you. Above all, I want this gown to catch the air of death in its folds, I want a small murder to be sewn into the hush of its hem, I want you, my quiet seamstress, as my accomplice. You must help me choose which of my many creatures must go, which of my selves is trickery rather than truth. I am so used to beguiling sisters, husband, lover, that I am disguised even to myself. Your part will be to listen to me as you sew. As you pin and tuck and alter, you will catch from my lips little snippets of truth, twisted threads of my quirks, the stubborn selvage of my Bear, my Swine, my Crow, and from all of these, I am persuaded, you will be able to assemble my salvaged self, Caroline Lamb, undisguised.

Will you accept that ragged remnant as your fee for my murder? Good. Let us start by taking your scissors to my bridal gown.

THE WEDDING SONG

It was when my chair scraped backwards away from my wedding feast with a screech that stopped the song in the castrato's throat—as you soon shall hear—that I first knew for sure I must hide myself from my husband and his milk-white mind, hide from him all marks of the dark maze where my thoughts bred like squirming clumps of mice.

My milk-white dress stitched for the Lamb. Remember? Too white. Even during the wedding ceremony my mind had begun to wander away from the Lamb, through my maidenhood's maze, calling to the creatures that had prowled and burrowed in the wilfulness of my childhood. My husband tried to recall my thoughts to him, grasping my hand in his as surely as a book closes itself about a straying word. He smiled the Lamb smile at me with such an assumption of peace between us that my cat's heart began to splutter and spit. I saw in his smile that his slippered life would seek to smooth away my spitting bundle of creatures and quirks and leave me quietly underfoot, under Lamb. No! My bundle shuddered, protested, and one unruly quirk broke loose.

I closed my eyes, blotting out the priest, and saw to my joy that it was the Swine who had broken loose in my maze, rooting in a humus of dank and rotting leaves, its own eyes closed in blissful satisfaction. Its skin had turned pearly white, with bristles glistening pure as snow. There was a brocade of torn leaves clinging to its underbelly.

(Ah, smutted Swine, Beast of defiance since my infancy!)

All through the vows, the Swine in its Muck accompanied me, its snout busy turning up with relish the topsoil of my desires, and I listened to its guttural breathing as the priest opened his mouth and I smiled at its squealing hymn of pleasure. So, we were married, my Swine to his Lamb.

At the wedding feast, as the Swine rolled about in the stench of feasts and battles long history in my mind, my distaste for my husband's meek neatness grew, and grew. I had drunk a little too much. They had served the pigeon and pomegranate and my thoughts swayed perhaps to the swooning and fretting of strings in the cornered octet. As I held a forkful of pigeon to my mouth, the pomegranate's red juice dripped onto my bodice. Dribbled. I heard the Swine grunt and snuffle and I aloud burbled, laughed. I turned my breast to my husband: 'Look, love, a hog of your own!'

There came a silence. The octet died. Lamb my husband blushed red and turned his face from me. Quite away. He dabbed at his mouth with a napkin—they all saw this—and pursed his lips as he sipped a little water. He would not look at me. He put his napkin down. He beckoned to the castrato. 'Sing for my bride my ode to the sweetness of her heart!' he said, but he would not look at me. I felt a drop of shame boil up into a rage. I clenched my fists. I glared at the spot where the castrato must stand.

(This is where Virgilio della Roccia stands before me like a rag doll stuffed with the silk of other people's songs and opens his mouth wide but in the long obstructed moment of my fury can summon nothing of love but a void: this is where the hushed hall is filled with the screech of my chair.)

I shut my eyes. I had been struck through. The Swine

squealed, heaving itself up with scrabbling terror, and disappeared into the miry blackness. Gone from me, expunged with a dab of napkin. I felt my heart beating. I could not imagine happiness. I opened my eyes and looked at my hands and saw how horribly large and white they were. I lumbered to my feet and left the room.

Smirks followed me a little way and then left me alone.

I brushed against a serving boy, passed through an arch and came to a small courtyard. At its far corner was a blue door. I crossed the courtyard, opened the blue door, and entered.

I found myself in a small but elegant room, a salon, its walls papered a mossy green. There were lilies in a glass bowl above the fireplace, white smutted with gold. In the centre of the room, sitting on its haunches, was a bear, black and russet, a poor stunted thing, muzzled and shackled and chained. He turned to look at me and I saw how his rheumy eyes wept.

In that moment, we recognised each other.

Lying in front of the fire, curled on the carpet, was a stranger, a gypsy man, deep in sleep. His cap had fallen off his head and his mouth hung open to show his rotting teeth. There was a cloak flung over him, patched and tattered and brindled with colour. His hands, twitching about his face, were grimy and calloused. He shuddered in his sleep and the cloak rose and fell as though it were a frayed, soiled map troubled by mountains restless beneath its paper skin.

I saw the cloak and I closed the door behind me.

My heart quietened in the moss green room. My sadness leaked out of me. I heard the little intimate sounds of our stillness: the gypsy's whistling breath, the slight chinking of the bear's chain, my own stomach gurgling. It seemed as though this odd proximity—a worn-out, snoring gypsy, a forlorn bear, a bride with a boiling heart—this conjunction held greater promise of joy than my own wedding vows. Ah! But I wished I might have such a pelt, such a lair for hiding, a way of journeying, as the gypsy's cloak.

And so I took it. I stole his cloak as he slept, lifting it away from him, slowly—crumpling his guise to my heart— stopping on afterthought to drop my diamond earrings into his cap.

The bear watched me, tilting his head thoughtfully as though weighing my gift against my theft.

In the small courtyard was a simple fountain. I closed the blue door behind me, held the cloak bundled in my arms, and stood listening to the singing and gushing of the water.

From behind the fountain appeared the song doll, Virgilio, stitched of the finest rags, his eyebrows embroidered with astonishment, his lips caught shyly in a French knot and his eyes dyed with darkness. His head tilted sadly as a rag doll's will, and I thought that he might call me by name. He opened his mouth, I heard him take a breath, and he lifted one hand in a gesture deftly sewn with consolation.

How can a doll stuffed with so much silk understand that it is a sad thing to have a heart? I wondered a little angrily, thinking to ignore him when he spoke. But the castrato was mute, and stood simply watching me, the bride both gift and theft, bundling in her arm a map of escapes.

I walked past him as though he wasn't there and passed from the courtyard into a corridor, looking for a place to hide what I had stolen.

But even as I was looking for a place to hide what I had stolen, I was pursued by the thought that I might send Virgilio della Roccia a note one day so that I might in private hear the voice that I had heard of, but had not heard.

WHAT I HAVE STOLEN

I slipped out of the bridal bed when I was sure that my husband had fallen asleep. On bare feet, I crept to my dressing room and pulled out the cloak from the hatbox where I had crammed it. I held up its folds to my face and breathed in its smells of food and sweat and smoke and bear-sorrows; spreading it over my bed, I admired it in the moonlight—its wily patches, its cunning embellishments, its manifold islands stitched with lore.

I took off my nightdress, letting it drop to the floor, and wrapped the cloak about me. It hung heavily from my shoulders, it surrounded me with its smell. Rich was my robe. I glanced at the mirror, sure now of magic.

And this is what I saw:

You, Madame Picot, couturiére, clad in oyster grey. You stand by a gibbet. All is dark but held by your fingers a silver needle shines, and swinging from the gibbet, cold and slender and gleaming, is a naked corpse. How beautiful the body is, slight as a maiden but as promising of strength as a youth. Turning and dangling in the dimness, it shows me the grace of its back but not the tenderness of its sex. One two, one two, it swings as the bear might dance or the doll, singing, might sway. You, Madame Picot, wrap the body about in an ashen cloth. Out flashes the silver shard of your scissors and, its noose cut through, the corpse slumps against your body. You stumble against its weight, and then right yourself. Your cheeks shine with tears. You ease the corpse to the floor, cradling its head against your bosom. One of its pale arms dangles across your lap. From out of your bag you pull a reel of the blackest of raven threads and pass it through the eye of the needle. (It is within your

24

gift to pass the blackest of raven hearts through the eye of your needle, Madame Couturiére.)

Picking up a raw edge of the grave cloth, you begin to sew.

Under the thrust and arc of your silver needle and with the tug and slip of your thread, the shroud begins to change. First, it blushes with the hues from the throat of a finch, warm and gay, and the cloth's weft gives way to the soft blur of feathers. The cloth ripples, a dark serpent in bright grass, a leaping fish cheating the water of its dominion. Feathers give ways to scales. You sew on, Madame Picot, smoothing and pleating and turning the cloth inside out. The scales harden and shine and I see that you have woven chainmail, armour, with breastplate and helmet. The soldier sleeps, dreaming in your arms, his cheek still soft with youth and his mouth both beautiful and resolute. You have fashioned his armour from the wondering breath of his childhood, his heart is a marvellous citadel under siege. You have given him passion for a sword and the emblem on his shield is of a red bear dancing in a field gold with lilies. It is my emblem.

Mine!

I lean closer to the mirror. When he stirs and wakes from his dream, I shall see if the soldier's eyes, Mme Picot, are also mine.

So on my wedding night, as I stood cloaked before the mirror (a soft creature shivering within a torn pelt, my bear's odour silvered and soiled by the secretive trickle where the moonlight ventured between pale thighs, there where my husband had discharged his fears into my venereal darkness), as I looked into the mirror and met my own eyes, I resolved that I should wage battle with the Lamb, defy all curfews to break my citadel's siege, and with my quirks, wrest from life a love worth some degree of death.

THE POET AND THE PIGLET

All that's best of bright and dark—that where rancour spills, the very scars shall sing!—all that's best of bright and dark came my way, over water, in Cumbria, one gloaming.

Ankle-deep and damp with mizzle, I stood watching, and the pebbles pressed themselves into my soles, seeking wounds on my honeymoon, my white feet smutted green by their soft bloom. Booted and boated and borne by the wind, he was there on the lake and gone in the gloom, and I saw what they said of the poet the lord the rogue was true, that bright and dark did meet, in that aspect.

Spying on him, I decided that the rebel Byron would be my lover, a wild rebuke to my timorous Lamb.

I contrived—hard—to meet him in the city, to corner him in the parlours and salons. I threw myself at him, for I was not wise. And fear hastened me, for I knew that I was no sister to Byron's beauty.

I threw myself at him: I was not wise. He caught me by the wrist at one of Circe's revels, and tugged at me. I followed him too readily. I was enfolded in a chamber as sweet as a damask rose, alone with my lord's honey tongue. It was I who buzzed, busily the grateful bee: not he. With his languorous smile, he asked me if I desired him, and nothing but yes, yes, did I buzz.

Too eagerly did the Bee wrestle with the sweet heads of Death's weeds.

I wore a brooch which I unpinned and laid as a pledge in his palm. He tossed it up, caught it and pocketed it. I saw a shadow pass behind the ardent shine of his eye.

History would name that shadow Boredom, but I named it Peril, and loved it at once.

My brooch was an octopus, small as a farthing, coiled suckingly upon itself, tenacious and tender in its groping. I was hoping he would pin it close to his heart.

But he dropped it in his pocket, and forgot it.

MY OCTOPUS HEART

I did not forget how I loved the octopus: the single dome of desire, the many contriving arms, all contained within a farthing's dot. My farthing's art and octopus heart had come to my cradle when I was a bald and squalling baby. My sister the golden Pandora took me and hid me in a closet and in my place swaddled a spotted piglet. The trick was not discovered until my mother plucked the piglet out to suckle it, but by then I had slumbered two hours amongst pomanders dusted with orris root, breathing the dreams of an extinguished changeling, and my heart had began to sprout its own limbs.

I have been richly spotted with trickery and quick to contrive ever since.

QUIETLY

One night in June when the air was warm and the house full of flowers, my husband frightened me awake. He was standing next to my bed, watching my face as I slept, and his awful quietness penetrated my dreams as a cloud of grey moths descending upon my face and throat and chest so thickly that it was difficult to breathe. 'I am trying to sing,' I complained to the moths and woke to find my husband's fingers touching my throat where the veins flutter and the breath sucks. I slapped his hands away and realised he was my husband and not a dream. 'Go back to bed and sleep', I mumbled at him.

It was he who was struggling to breathe, not me. Silent sobs rose to his throat to be pulled down again. He was surrounded by tiger lilies, poppies, daffodils blaring wide open—flowers sent to me by my lover, all stained and streaked strangely by the moon's ghostly juice. 'These—' my husband cried, swinging his hand at the prowling lilies, 'these—these—these—'

'These are nothing.' I got out of bed and put my arms around his shoulder. 'They are harmless. This is just silly, darling.'

My husband went out of my room without speaking another word.

THE HALF SISTER

There were times that I paid Byron's debts with my own money, with Lord Lamb's, until coins became tangled and purses bewitched by his charms beyond recall. Ah, but it was warm with him in my bed.

'Byron.' I curled one of his dark curls about my finger. 'Shall I come to Augusta's ball? Lamb will not, so I would go alone.'

He rolled away from me and yawned. 'It is nothing to me.'

'But you will be there?' The Bear beseeched its chain.

'Probably not. Sounds to me like it will be a dead bore.'

I sat up in the bed and wrapped my arms around my knees. 'Augusta seems to be annoyed with me.'

'Probably she is. My sister is annoyed with everybody at times.'

'But particularly with me. I could swear that she looked at me with a sneer yesterday.'

'Undoubtedly.'

'Has she said anything?'

'Why should we talk about you? I probably wouldn't remember it, anyway.' He frowned at the ceiling. 'That colour is repulsive, you know.'

'I don't think I will go. I don't think she wants me there.'

'Good. I would call that shade of pink a sickly tone.'

My glance strayed down his beautiful lean body and rested for a moment upon his foot, disguised in bandages. The spot where a worm begins to foul the rose. I stood up and crossed the room and knew without looking that, for the first time, Byron did not follow with eyes curious to see my body walk in its nakedness.

I was consoled in that little loss by Virgilio, who visited me the same day and sang me a lullaby in his sister's voice.

AMARETTI

Every second Thursday of the month at nine in the evening, we nine women would meet for supper and poetry and slander: Oriole, Augusta, Adelaide, Julia, Eulalie, Olivia, Calliope, Rosalind, and myself. A winding, coiling, crushing octopus with Augusta Leigh as its head. We were an uneasy, whispering sisterhood. Our minds ground the bitter green of our secret thoughts to produce poems like little white cakes of almond flesh, amaretti, on the edge of sweetness, on the edge of poison. We would admire with tongues that sang and lips that spat; we would clap with fingers clever with caresses and palms dug with the crescent wounds of nails driven by envy. I loved Circe's Circle: a chamber where I could distil my passions and squirt the voluptuous ink of poetry over my lust, my sadness, my infidelity, while my husband's gentle smile curdled in my memory.

I took Virgilio della Roccia with me to the Circle in the month of June: I flung him amongst the tentacles as though he were a soft-bellied, spawnless fish. I thought that Circe would be hungry only for his voice and, stupidly, I did not stop to think what a curious morsel his flesh might be. Oh but the octopus is a soft and sucking-footed mother whose dome hides a ruthless beak. Augusta Leigh was gimlet-eyed and swollen with beauty as she watched Virgilio sing Orpheus. Her fingers traced the satin on her bodice and she glanced at me and she smiled.

I did not immediately wonder.

CONSOLATION

Nor did I wonder that my husband's melancholy had grown so dark. They were all ill in the head in his family, all too moddled and coddled in their sadness. His sighs exhausted me. Did he know I was unfaithful? Probably, yes, certainly. I did not care. He was in my mind a shrinking mannikin, whereas Byron the lover, the poet, the warrior, the rogue's power to deal me life and death grew all the while.

At first when we made love, it was poetry without wounds. At first when we made love, I believed that I was his one true infidelity. He would lay me quite bare, and run his hands up and down my body. I remember that now, when I am alone at night. How his warm, smooth hands stroked my thighs and brushed lingeringly past my waist to make me shiver. How he would watch my face with interest and then how he would smile. And when he smiled, how giddily buzzed the sipping Bee about his lips.

That all changed. The warmth, the smile. Required some effort from him. Cajoled by my unease. One day he flicked the point of my elbow with his finger, and then pulled away from me. Turned his face to look up at my hateful ceiling. I whispered his name and in the glance that answered me I saw how my body was distorted in his eye, bloated in the middle, a woman's muddle of humps.

Straightaway he closed his eyes and began to hum. He got up and dressed himself, still humming, and hid his beautiful foot and his ugly foot in his boots. He left, and for hours I could not move from my bed. I was fixed to it by the rope knotted inside my throat.

Alarmed that I might be unwell, my husband came into my room. I remained where Byron had left me, in my muddled nakedness, staring at the pink skin of the ceiling. The Lamb nudged with his timid nose around the reasons for my desolation, but did not budge my feelings one inch. I did not speak, I did not whisper, I did not moan or sigh. I gave him no reason to hope that my silence might be wedded to his melancholy, and so he left my room more lonely and unwedded than when he entered it. (I have many memories that make me wince for shame.)

The day darkened and grew cold. I curled up amongst my bedclothes. I felt like a creature pulled out of its shell, pale and repulsive upon a miserable beach. My maid came and murmured that the castrato had come for our lesson, and I said, 'Show him in.'

So it was that Virgilio bent over me and stroked my hair and told me the story of his sister's lullaby.

A NEST OF KNIVES

Suor Tommaso del Dubbio wore a black habit and strode within its confines with an angry purpose. Suor Tommaso del Dubbio wore boots of thick black leather with heavy heels that thumped scars into the earth where she passed. Suor Tommaso del Dubbio lived in a convent in the town where Virgilio della Roccia's father earned his keep catching rats. Suor Tommaso del Dubbio was the eldest, angriest daughter of an influential Venetian family who prided themselves on their patronage of music and poetry. Suor Tommaso del Dubbio came sometimes to the church where Virgilio sang in the choir, and Suor Tommaso del Dubbio—in the winter that Virgilio turned eight, *l'inverno del mio dolore*—came to visit the ratcatcher with a pouch heavy with coins and a mouth redolent of miracles. The Lord had sent her to rescue Virgilio's voice from manhood, and she would herself pay for the operation out of her love for sacred music. And so she seduced poverty.

Little Raffaela della Roccia, then nine years old, crouched against the door, listening through the darkness to la Suora's seduction. Raffaela came creeping to Virgilio in the bed that the little ones shared, and nestled her hands around his face like two warm, blind puppies. Raffaela told Virgilio that la Suora meant to take him to sing before l'Arcivescovo and il Duca and would keep him in a cage. But Raffaela whispered to him to have no fear; in the morning he must hide in Signor Benvenuto's loft and she would cut off her hair and dress in his clothes and la Suora would suspect nothing until she took the knife to find that this quail had lain no eggs, and Raffaela would scamper home, free.

She sang to him of a boat on the sea and Virgilio fell asleep in her arms.

That last morning, Raffaela did indeed hack off her copper curls and clad herself in his breeches, but her deceit was no equal to the nun's needle-like eyes. So it was that she wept in the dust as Virgilio rode away beside the brooding nun in her black carriage. They reached the city and Suor Tommaso took Virgilio to a room at the back of a house where the air was as dejected as brown and stagnant water. There stood a thin, tall man with creaking hands, dressed in doleful black clothes, with a bowl of knives and a narrow smile.

'This is il Dottore,' said the nun. 'He is the man who will save your voice from corruption. Do not give him any trouble. I pray that when you are famous you remember to thank God for your good fortune here today.'

And so it was that the slenderness of Virgilio's throat was preserved while all else was lost.

'Why did you tell me that story?' I looked up into Virgilio's face, at his soft and crinkled skin, the long, aunt-like cheeks, the pouch of fat tucked beneath his chin, and his graceful, powdery throat.

'I want you to know how brave my sister was. For her, love was simple, like the rain, but for you,' my teacher scolded me but his eyes were warm, 'love is as dirty as a trampled puddle.'

'We are talking about different things. She was a child. A sister is not a wife or a lover.'

'Ah! So you flick her aside—pff!—just like Suor Tommaso did the day she took me.'

I sidestepped him. 'You must hate that woman.'

'La Suora? Must I?' The ragged doll was suddenly fierce with sly questions. 'How can I hate la Suora and yet love my voice?'

I decided it was pointless to talk to my teacher of love;

a man with his incapacity must be innocent of its difficulties and disguises.

THE TWO POETS

You have spilt your pins, Madame: did something in my story distract you? Look, all over the carpet and under your stool, you will have to stoop. (I glance in the mirror and I see Raffaela crouching to pluck her bright shining tears from the sienna dust, so that they might not prick the feet of those who trample them.)

In my hands, pins are dull and nasty things, but for you they will hold together awkward shapes to make beauty new. This gown now begins to flow like a song. You cluck your teeth and shake your head when I spill my story of pride and anger and envy. I am sorry, Madame Picot, but they are the only pins I have to hold my passions together.

But what about your quirks? you ask me, trimming the frays. Quirks are pins, no?

Yes, Madame, quirks are pins, you are quick to understand. Let me tell you what happened the day after I broke my husband's heart with my silence.

I went to the masque alone, for I did not think that Lamb would come. I wore a bear's face and the gypsy's cloak and my limbs were chained. In between dances a wolf came up to me, a black wolf with silver tears stuck to his face. It spoke to me. 'Do you want to know who is Byron's lover?' it said and I felt sick for it was my husband's voice. 'Then watch carefully. It is the pirate.' And the wolf slunk away.

I watched carefully and I waited for the moment when the masks came down, when Columbines became men, and leopards, women. My own mask dropped, but my chains stayed. The pirate, I saw with a greedy glance, was Augusta Leigh, swaggering with loveliness. I ran shambling from the masque, my eyes rheumy with weeping. The Lamb was waiting for me at home, ready with comfort, but I slammed my door in his face. I stayed awake, listening to the murmurings of Augusta and Byron in my mind, tumbling amongst ink-dark sheets like moons coupling, absorbed in reflected beauty.

The next morning, I went straightaway to find Byron, to throw my knowledge in his face. I heard the murmurings as I came closer to his room, but when I looked in, it was not Augusta, but a different moon altogether, bright in Byron's shadow. That Byron should pour his love into that other poet—how beautifully gleamed the skin of their backs and their buttocks as I spied them clasping together, shuddering and gasping in the blinking morning light—that he should press his charm into such a cleft, bewildered me. How could this be—a man?

I hurried to hide from the sounds of their love-making, and I found myself crouching on all fours, gasping, whimpering, the beaten dog, behind some bushes in the garden.

I thought: I have turned myself inside out to please him and it comes to nothing, it comes to this, that after a while a woman's body turns from poetry to prose and she is a more sure source of disappointment to a man than his own mirror. What sort of secrets does this creature keep once she has crawled into his bed naked?

What sort of secrets does this creature keep? I asked myself with pale shock. What sort of secrets does this creature keep?

Around and around the question buzzed and after a while it lulled me and even cheered me so that I sat down and wiped the tears with my hem.

I hummed Raffaela della Roccia's lullaby and thought of her shorn head.

I smiled and saw that, one yard away, a crow stood watching me, a daunting perspicacity in her eye.

I admired her black widow's weeds.

I admired the tufts of her black breeches, their elegant sheen. Her breeches put in mind Raffaela's reckless trick.

BREECHES

That was when I came to you, Madame Picot, with my request for one shirt in finest lawn, a waistcoat in silk, dark as juniper berries, a coat in olive-green broad cloth with revers of soft russet silk, a white lawn neckcloth, and breeches raven black.

And breeches raven black.

(That was when I came to you and felt the silver shard of your scissors slice the rope that caught my throat, that caught my sex. That was when I came to you and you cradled my head against your bosom and showed me in the mirror the possibilities of new birth.)

HIS CLUB FOOT

I went to him one more time, myself a poet of disguise, a pilgrim soldier, my own rogue lover. I stood before him in the richness of my fine and heavy coat. I took off my top hat and with my walnut stick, I knocked a little mud off the sides of my riding boots. I did not swagger, for I felt no need; my costume had sufficient eloquence.

(Look at me, Byron, I have stepped into that world

where poets' minds glide over the rhythm of their bodies. Test me and see how well I belong.)

He lay back—he did not come close and touch as I had hoped. He asked me to take off my boots, my coat, my waistcoat—slowly. Slower. Yes—now, stop!

I stood before him in my shirt and stockings, with my breeches half down. I could hear his breathing and the world suddenly seemed too quiet. A cat was complaining outside, rubbing herself against the door. I felt my sadness, leaking. He beckoned, so I lay down beside him, and he took me from behind. He was not entirely rough. I did not quite know what to make of it, but I must say that I did enjoy it, in an uncomfortable sort of way, for part of the time. But afterwards, quickly afterwards, I began to feel embarrassed. I waited for his hands to soothe me, to wipe away the hot blush, and when at last I felt them stirring over me, I felt a little happiness.

But even then, they were my clothes he stroked, and not my skin, my arms, my hidden breasts. I thought that I might cry. I pretended to sleep. His hands dropped down, and he was soon asleep. I listened to the distant song of a small bird, desolate in the grey dusk.

I dressed myself, even to putting on my boots and tying my neckcloth. Moving gently so as not to wake him, I knelt on the bed, next to his feet. I lifted his left foot, his deformity, and held it in the cradle of my hands.

(Remember Pandora's trick? Remember me swaddled and closed in a closet, dusted with orris, the powdered root of death? I think it was the odour of darkness that tempted me to unwind the bandage.)

The bandage was clean white and soft, crêpe two inches in width and about five feet long. I wondered if it was there to cushion the foot from pain, or to disguise the details of his deformity from his lovers, or whether the two were one.

When the last turns dropped down, I held his bare foot with my bare hands, wanting for an instant to fling it away from me. The skin was soft and very pink, peeling in places. There was a faint, moist, almost putrid odour. It might have been an aborted piglet in my cradled hands, limp and misshapen. The foot was sharply turned in, creating a tender, macerated cleft where the inner arch should have been. The toes curled about themselves, the nails cutting into the flesh. There was a ridge of callous where his weight was borne, and a round shallow ulcer was developing over one of the bony protuberances, ruby red with a rim of creamy yellow.

I supported his foot with hands trembling with tenderness and, well, revulsion, as though it had dropped from my own womb to make me doubt the love that had seeded it. This was what my lover had been at such pains to hide, the little crippled sole, the ugly sore that made his Beauty limp, the foot that he would never forgive.

With one hand I began to strike the foot, as gently as once I had been used to stroking his face. First, I touched the top of his foot where it curved with such terrible strain. I touched the helpless, twisted toes, parting them with my little fingertip so that they might know a moment's relief. I touched the ridge, circling the ulcer. I touched the concavity of the outer arch where the blue-green veins could be seen to branch beneath satin-white skin. And then—with the same mixture of hesitation and compulsion which a youth might suffer when he first fingers a moist vulva—I touched his pink cleft. The foot twitched violently, withdrew, and relaxed.

His eyes flew open. He sat up, pulling his foot away from me, throwing a corner of the quilt over it. He was pale, his eyes were dark.

'You are sick,' he said to me, 'Lady Lamb.'

Wordlessly, I held the bandage out to him (he would not take it from me, so I dropped it on the bed), and wordlessly, I left his apartment for the deepening dusk.

Straightaway, still in my raven breeches and my olive coat, I sought Virgilio out. I found him behind a blue door—I heard his voice pour out on to the street, incorrupt as glass, wilful as thrumming metal—and burst upon him in his precarious room woven through and through with the winding of cats, the shivering of moths, the scent of old oranges softening within skins powdered with mould. He was wrapped about in a silk gown mottled and speckled brown and gold, like a pomander sticky with orris and tied about the middle with a sash. Singing, he soared, high and fast and pure and strong, then he saw me and stopped. His lips parted, astonished at my disguise, at my theft of his sex, at my face swollen with tears.

'You have lost something, Lady Lamb?'

'I have lost Byron.' I wiped my nose on my rich sleeve.

'You expect to find him here?' The doll looked coldly at the manly figure I cut.

'Imbecile! I have lost what I loved!' I stamped a foot so hard that a striped cat shrank spitting into a corner.

'Have you? Really? What you loved, you say?' He folded his arms, watching me as though he saw through a Lady better than a Freak ought.

'Yes, damn you, you heard! I've turned myself inside out and nothing he sees in me pleases him.'

'You thought you might please him with these panto-mime breeches?'

I looked away. 'Raffaela was no pantomime.'

'Ah, but a sister is not a wife or a lover.'

For a moment I thought that I might slap him, slap his soft cheeks with my large hand, for daring to speak my own words back at me. Instead I muttered, surly as a bear, 'What would you know?' It was as good as a slap.

I made for the door, but he came after me and caught me. I turned my head, thinking he would be the one to slap me, but there was no slap. He wrapped his arms about me so that I was sheltered in the slumbering sweetness of his gown, and touched my ear with his lips and tickled me with his questions. I listened as a conch shudders and sighs from its core of emptiness when the little raw salty creature inside has died. 'What does it matter if Byron finds you boring? Is it so awful if your pride must bleed and die a little from this cut? Will nothing else inside you survive its death?' He rocked me to and fro, a boat bobbing by Raffaela's lullaby shore.

'It is not a matter of pride.' I fought him a little.

'What, then?'

'Things will be dull without him.' I felt myself sinking. 'You think me very shallow, don't you?'

'I think you swim in a very shallow circle, Lady Octopus. What goes around, comes around, they say of circles.'

I stared at him. 'You mean Circe? I don't call that shallow. We are sisters. There is something special between us.'

'Indeed. Which your sisters have been kind enough to pass on to me.' And his smile was bitter-sweet.

I frowned as though puzzled. 'What are you talking about? A secret gift?'

'A sickness, Lady Lamb. A disease that particularly travels in circles.'

'A sickness?' My mind stumbled. 'You have been lovers? Nobody told me. Who have you slept with? We have no secrets. With Augusta? Tell me! Who else? How many of them?' My face was hot with a mixture of jealousy and shame at my own foolishness. I saw that he would not answer me. I pulled away from him. I stood tall in my fine coat and fine boots. I thrust my hands into the pockets of my breeches. 'Very well, then. Explain it to me, this sickness that you say some of our circle shares.'

I turned and looked at him defiantly, but inside I was quailing in my most hidden nook, praying that there was no explanation to hear and no disease to fear. He untied his sash and the gown dropped from his shoulders. His head nodded above his body, a naked doll joined with springs. So I looked at the little breasts of sagging fat, the long slope of his womanly belly, the triangle of tendrils. There it was above the savaged purse which was long and arched and quivering in its ivory sheath, soft as kid. He watched me as I looked more closely, both the irony and the smile gone from his face.

I saw the unwholesome marks on his skin, little garnets scattered on his ivory foreskin, bejewelling thickly his breasts, his belly, the palms of his hands. Silvery patches showed amidst his dark curling hair, dainty erosions amongst his eyebrows. And where his corona peeped at me, rosy and gleaming, was the painless corrosion from which the disease had crept, an ulcer deep like the setting from which a diamond had been lost. A wound placed there by a sister of Circe, in answer to the wound placed below by a daughter of Christ.

I heard a little noise which took me by surprise: it was me, crying with my own voice, dismayed at the cleverness of Death who had found out where my heart was hid, while my pride made me look elsewhere.

I went home late that night and kissed my sleeping husband with the little store of ruined feeling I had left for him. I went to my room and flung open the doors of my fabulous wardrobe. Costume after costume I tried on, until darkness became dawn and, each time I turned to see myself in the mirror, I saw that in my image there was still more pride than I could unpick.

You came to me that morning, and you cut me clothes from a very plain cloth, and there was nothing fancy in the manner of your stitches.

THE RATCATCHER'S DAUGHTER

It was the last Thursday of Virgilio's life, before the doctor cured his syphilis by poisoning his body. Three sacks of rats I lugged to Circe's castle. Byron was there, surrounded by eight sucking feet. (Do not think that I was still pursuing him, then.) Eight women with candles aflame, fingers sticky with marchpane, breath sweet with canary wine, the circle crissed and crossed with the guile of their eyes.

I wore grey breeches and a drab coat. My sacks struggled in the dimness, obscure but not mute.

'Caro!' Julia rose. 'We had given you up for dead, my sweet!' There was a fragment of cake on her lip, spotted black with poppy seed.

'Beyond the Styx,' averred Oriole, another seed caught between her teeth.

They had yellow teeth, all of them, spotted with Morpheus' seeds, as they turned to smile. In their eyes I saw reflected not myself but lewd suggestions, pods without seeds, sockets without orbs, the coinless purses furtive in their own hearts. And I had called this poetry! I dropped the sacks down and I heard the outrage of the rats.

'Yes, I have been dying. We are all dying, of ourselves. Our necrologue, ladies!' Your scissors flashed through the twine. And like the Styx pouring out from the Dog's three ruthless heads, the rats streamed out in sewered colours, twisting about themselves, claws scrabbling over snouts in haste and fury. A spotted motley, they spread and swarmed over carpet and furniture, across the skittering oak table, amaretti fouled and canary spilling. Squealing, they swung themselves up on curtains and skirts, splattering brocade and sarsenet with the hot angry urine of their captivity.

I trembled, weakened and spent by the outflowing of my fury. I returned home with my empty sacks, and wondered how I could begin to repair my life, such as it was.

FITTING

This is a good gown, Madame Picot, exquisite and penitent and without guile. Your good heart has divested it of the envy and vengefulness of my early design. I am glad of that, for loss finds no solace in thieving. Today I bury someone dear, and this gown is right for mourning.

This shall be my gown for journeying, now that my teacher is gone. I mean to travel the long road to Ravenna, and from there travel to the city where there is a house where the air is as dejected as brown water. From that house I shall travel in a brooding black carriage to a town where a girl crouches to pick her tears out of the road, a child shorn of merriment.

I want to see what good I can do on that road.

I thank you for your faithful industry. I thank you for your wise craft. Your inventions are devoid of fraud. Your gift is rich.

In this purse, are your guineas.

Silhouette

GILLIAN MEARS

I went home with her because her brother had died. Venetia said he was cremated a week after the accident, on Venetia's thirty-fifth birthday. She was so beautiful that the ruined skin around her eyes didn't matter. If anything, that kind of ruin added to her kind of beauty. I didn't care that she felt it important to lie about the age she had turned the day of her brother's funeral or that later that night, there was a ledge of grey in the otherwise black hair between her legs.

The brother died the day I arrived in France; a hot holiday day, with a storm breaking on the river at Pont Marie as I hauled my suitcase up the Metro steps. The handle of my suitcase broke and the sweat soaked my shirt so much that when I looked down, I could see the dark shape of my nipples through the white cotton. The first graffiti postcard I bought from one of the stalls on the Quai said *l'insolence de l'ete me tu qu il neige*. The insolence of summer is killing me, if only it would snow. The writing was black and stencilled onto an old white wall that was peeling to orange and I kept forgetting to send it to my girlfriend in Australia.

The night I met Venetia at the Nok, it was so hot there'd been another storm at midnight. The air felt dark green with storminess, as if even as one storm ended there might be another one sweeping up the Seine. I hadn't anticipated that Paris could feel so tropical. My clothes were always too warm. In my first week I had to shave under my arms.

The Nok bar is halfway along rue Keller. It would've been just another unremarkable street behind Bastille, ending in a high school, except for the resemblance of my face graffitied twice onto a panel of wall.

I had found my face the day I first came to look in daylight for the bars, holding the map a bookseller in rue Sainte Croix de la Bretonnerie had drawn for me. I held the hand-drawn map as inconspicuously as I could. Behind large, solid timber doors carved with faces, I heard the sighs I felt sure were the sighs of naked French girls lying together. Although the windows were empty of faces, I had the sensation that mocking eyes were looking down on the stupid Australian girl who was trying to hide her map, even as she followed it.

If the face on the wall wasn't my face exactly, it was very similar: dark eyes and protrudent ears and the same thin hair hanging over one eye. The face had been sprayed onto the wall using a stencil and the artist had utilised the texture and colour of the wall in order to create effects of lightness and shadow. Seeing this face on the wall that could've passed for my own, on my first week in Paris, when there were no numbers on any of the doors that might or might not have been bars by night, made me feel sad. Even the smell of the street became sad. In the increasing heat of the day it had the smell of old, abandoned bird cages, the colourful birds long dead, and all that is left, a glimpse of tail feather in a curl of the yellowing newspaper which used to line the bottom.

On the night I met Venetia, I pressed the buzzer of the° door which by then I knew was the right one. I looked down at the boots I'd bought in London in such a hurry. I remembered my pleasure which turned to pain. How small they'd made my feet look; how after a month of walking around London, and considerable foot agony, both big toes finally burst through the leather uppers as I walked up the hill towards Hampstead one day.

Venetia was sitting at the bar and turned to look at me as I came through the door. She tapped the stool next to her stool so that even though I'd come to dance, I sat down instead. She was wearing a black, oversize jacket which made her shoulders look enormous but I could tell that underneath she was tiny. She had these tiny, fragile bones that matched the ones in her face. Quail bones, I thought. She would feel like quail bones. Her dark hair ringleted over her shoulders and was of the kind that only begins to grow from where the forehead has actually curved over. I have always loved women with high hairlines but there was something so childlike about her brown eyes, the hint of tears in them, that as I watched her face in the mirror at the back of the bar, I thought not about kissing the forehead but about putting my hand to it, as if to check for a temperature. She had a gap between her front teeth wide enough for another tooth. Her tongue, which came through the gap when she smiled, was a dark, glistening mauve.

After a while, other girls came up to the bar. They were very drunk and smelt of the damp walls of the dance cellar. Their skins were terrible.

'Kung ar Roo!' they said, hopping around. 'I'm the All Juicing Machine,' the girl with the worst acne kept repeating and only months later do I realise she was telling me she had an answering machine and trying to write her phone number onto the skin of my wrist.

One girl had hit her head on the narrow door lintel into the cellar and wanted Venetia to kiss it better, which she did, kissing the air delicately over the rising lump. She laughed at me then and I saw that her teeth also seemed slightly mauve, as if soaked in red wine.

'Your long fingernails,' I exclaimed at one point to Venetia.

'The men go wild over them,' she said, making a pattern in her glass with one.

'Men?' I said.

'Only very occasionally. And then they love me to scratch them.'

Most of the time in the bar, Venetia told me about her brother. 'These beads,' she said, lifting them from her throat, 'were my brother's love beads from a one-month horse ride in the Masai Mara in Kenya the year before. I know I must write something about him soon. He was exactly like you. You're on the same length of waves I think. It's amazing. On some nights my brother made a beautiful girl. No one would know the difference. He could trick anyone. Once, even me.'

When we reached Venetia's room, the dead brother's dog whipped around our ankles in excitement and pleasure. He was wearing a green coat sewn by Venetia from out of her brother's green corduroy jacket. She showed me a scar almost healed over on the dog's face. When I was given a little lick on the chin by the dog, Venetia said, in a voice full of affection, that she was not the only one to find a resemblance.

Before we went to bed she wanted me to have a moustache. She selected a dark-brown eyeliner so soft she hardly had to press. When I protested, she said, 'Ah-ah, uh-uh,' and pulled me back into a sitting position on the bed. The silvery down already there above my top lip made her tender. She cooed at my moustache au naturelle, pressing the pencil in small downward strokes. When she reached the indentation of skin underneath my nose she stopped to unbutton my shirt. She brushed the four fine hairs around my left areola and said it was exactly so with her brother. In the mirror she held up I saw that with the luxurious, near-black moustache, I looked more like a young man than ever before. At the same time my lips had become an obscene and lush shade of red. It also seemed to me that my teeth, only slightly protrudent in reality, had underneath their moustache become those of a buck rabbit.

Behind me, in the mirror, I could see Venetia undressing. The dog also watched from his basket in the corner, his soft brown eyes only occasionally looking my way. She was smooth brown all over but the skin on her thighs was stretched, suggesting she'd once carried much more weight or had a child, for on her breasts, too, which she pressed against my back, were similar striations.

She lead me, still clothed, to the bed. 'I have some photos,' she said.

The brother was androgynous and dark and not really so much like me except in the holiday in Africa when he too grew a moustache. In one photograph Venetia was looking with laughter at her brother who, against a backdrop of elephants and safari tents, was holding her nipple in solemn imitation of some famous European painting. I couldn't remember the name of the artist but I was able to laugh for Venetia, recognising the spoof. His fingertips only just held on to her nipple and the curve of his fingers formed an almost complete circle to the right of her breast. Venetia said they had been very dangerous. They had taken their bedding out of the safety of their tents and slept in the open. They had seen the ghostish, humped outlines of hyenas and heard lions mating.

When I began to brush my moustache along the skin of Venetia's thighs she let the photos and the sheets of paper that were the beginning of her story slide out of her hands. I heard them falling onto the floor, one by one at first and then in a rush. I went back to the soft skin underneath her knees. I licked Venetia under her knee and on the strong tendons there. She pulled me up higher. My hair hurt. She was tiny under my tongue; the smallest tip I kept losing. I wanted to lift my face up to hers; to tell her she was hurting my hair but her voice was carrying me too. I was making my tongue thick. I was making it round, trembling inside and pulling out and for the first time I heard his name.

In the morning, I thought at first I was home. There was a pot of yellow chrysanthemums in a tub at a window and I could hear the dark, sweetening starlings of my Melbourne childhood. Then Venetia was beside me, laughing and apologetic because in sleep my head had bumped against a wall of not-yet-dry yellow paint. The new paint was very ugly, with a swirl render. She made me a large breakfast cup of coffee and some tiny squares of white toast which she fed to the dog spread with unsalted butter. In daylight, she saw I was older after all than her brother; my Australian skin. I felt disheartened. I turned my face away from Venetia and looked outside to a stone angel I could see outside the window. The angle had a trumpet held aloft at his lips and when I stood up to see more clearly, I saw there were four angels, one at each corner of a building topped by a Byzantine, patterned dome. The leaves of the tree in front of the nearest angel were beginning to turn yellow. I saw that there was an actual twiginess at the top of the tree and that the stonework of the dome also looked flimsier, like wickerwork, as the sun lit up the eastern side. Venetia, coming up behind me but not touching, said that a silent order of nuns lived inside the building. Sometimes her little brother would try to shock them with his music or his naked body at the window but at such times the nuns always acted as if they were also blind and deaf.

'The Australian sun,' she said, touching the arrangement of dark freckles on my neck. 'You must always put on creams.' She rearranged her dressing gown, looking immaculate. Even her pubic hair looked combed and arranged, the ledge of grey as if tinted to highlight her dark lips.

By contrast I appeared deranged in the bathroom mirror and searched in vain up and down the floor-to-ceiling hair and skin cosmetics shelves for a headache tablet. The sadness in the sounds of plumbing in a building you know you'll never return to again. The smell of foreign soap. On the floor the dog's litter-tray was as immaculate as everything else. I opened a pot of eyecream full of collagen bubbles and dabbed it at the corners of my Australian eyes. I scrubbed at the moustache with some squares of pink toilet paper.

'Please,' she said urgently, when I came back out, still with yellow paint in my hair. 'Come with me now on my way to work?' She was dressed and slipping on black platform sandals.

'Could you help me get this off?' I said, indicating the remains of the moustache.

'But it is necessary. Wait,' she said and after removing the mess with moisturiser, redrew a complete and dark-brown moustache. Unlike the night before, she worked swiftly. 'Bon, allez,' she said.

'I can't go to work with you like this!'

'Not work. On the way. Come, come. You'll see.'

Even though I could still taste her in my mouth, even though I felt she must have dried all over my face, it was as if nothing intimate had ever existed between us. I wished I could speak more French, to re-establish something. 'C'est froid,' I said down on the street, wishing I could say how it seemed that the summer had passed in the night.

'At least the wind is broken,' Venetia replied.

'You say, the wind has died.'

'Oh,' she said. The light was stiff and cold around the black scarf she had wound around her neck. Then a little further along she turned to me, saying, 'My brother is dead and now you want to kill the wind, too. I didn't know Australians were meant to be so gloomy.'

'But broken. That's not a very happy word either. Broken-hearted.'

'Well this depends. Broken windows can be happy. Or, the storm has broken.' Venetia yawned. Her teeth were still mauve and looked like they should be polished.

We saw a woman in a black leather collar with studs. Her skirt was cut into an upside down V so that anyone looking there could just catch a glimpse of her golden-coloured hair. The man behind her pressed himself against her as she opened the door. They'd been walking a small, black dog wearing a miniature version of her collar. Before they disappeared inside, they turned around and laughed with a hint of disdain at me.

There were bits of pigeon in the carpark we were crossing, rotting in puddles. Not even the feral cats would eat them because they were so waterlogged. My shoe hit one and Venetia laughed ruefully at me.

'Where are we going?'

'If you don't mind, I would very much like to get your silhouette cut,' she said.

I had seen the silhouette cutters, cajoling tourists outside the Pompidou Centre immediately before the entrance doors at the front of the building and to one side of the Fat Man and his throng of watchers. But the cutter we arrived at was a loner. He had set up his stand not far from the Jardin du Carrousel's Arc de Triomphe, in amongst excavations to the newest Louvre extension work. Venetia greeted him as a friend. He found my appearance amusing. The moustache, the paint, my shoes with the holes. I must stand like so, he said. His display board pictured examples of American girls with hair-wanded locks and banged fringes. It wouldn't take him very long, so if I could please stay as still as possible. Venetia smiled encouragingly. She came over to tilt my chin up into a slightly more noble profile. I was facing in the direction of two winged women, giantesses in stone. These had been caged first in timber, close to their bodies and faces and nearly touching their wings; and then, as if they might still be dangerous, in a metal enclosure. The enclosure was full of weeds resembling little choko vines and French grasses. Some of the metal fencing was down at the edges from people staring or taking photos. The women in the cages had mossy hips and small yellow leaves had gathered in their laps. There were some lions too, not in cages, their stone bellies so eroded they looked like famine lions. A crane started up with a clank, its reflection deep red in the Louvre windows.

Although I only stood there for about twenty minutes, when I was allowed to move there were two silhouettes of my face. One for me and one for Venetia. One night she'd walked all the way to the other bar along from the Nok on the other side of the road. The imagined shadow of her brother's face crossing the wall in the headlights of a car had given her the idea of his face abroad in the city. Even though he was dead, his face could appear at all his favourite haunts. Venetia said the walls of the city were like a gallery already, with faces and messages and the names of the dead and the alive in tiny letters or in larger rap-graffiti writing. For Venetia some walls refused to be sad enough. A bump underneath where Venetia placed her little brother's mouth would make him wildly happy or the stain of water would cut through his face like a scar.

In my memory, I am standing there, looking at the profile of a delicate-faced boy. Venetia is next to me, saying isn't it a good likeness, but that now she must go. I am pressing my Australian addresses and phone number onto her, saying she must contact me if ever she comes to my city. I am all gawky, with a tuft of yellow paint in my hair, and the moustache I cannot quite accept, which as Venetia walks away, I'm already wiping off on the sleeve of my coat.

I tell my girlfriend when I come home and I can see immediately that she doesn't believe me.

'That has always been my fantasy,' she says. 'A French woman. Telling me the parts of my body in French.' And she handles the silhouette without the delicacy it requires, so that his nose has been torn and looks less beautiful now.

I tell my girlfriend that the autumn leaves in the garden remind me of her own delicate skin but in fact I find myself thinking more of Venetia's brother; the yellowness in my look-alike's eye whites; the mottles that spread into his high, girl cheekbones when he was drunk and alive with his laughter.

Venetia wanted so much to write about her little brother that maybe she has. *Accqude au silence tu peux crier les murs n'ght 'As D'Greilles* I read on her postcard, which pictures a graffitied wall. I have pinned it to my wall. Silence, you can scream the walls down.

There is no message other than the postcard's but I am sure it is from Venetia. I am sure, taking the card down to finger its edges, that I can feel her elegance in the way she has formed each letter of the word Melbourne. The stamp is a giant one from the philatelic section of a post office in the sixth arrondissement. It pays tribute to Rosa Bonheur with her most famous picture, *The Horse Fair*. When I look up Bonheur in an art book I read that she was an artist of the 1800s who, defying convention, dressed always in men's clothing. She ended up living to a fine old age in a chateau creatured with exotics from all over the known world. She particularly liked African animals, I read. There was a lion cub who played with a cheetah.

THE MAN FROM
THE CARIBBEAN

WILLIAM YANG

That morning he woke to the soft whirl of the overhead fan in a room of the Sea Breeze Guest House. Through the window, palm trees in the middle distance broke the view into vertical strips while a branch of frangipani laden with flowers thrust itself horizontally into the picture. There was no mistaking that the juices of the vegetation flowed more quickly in the tropics. The heavy fragrance of flowers hung in the room so that even to move, to get out of bed, he felt he was stirring the air like soup.

The man from the Caribbean, whose name was Carlos, dressed slowly, putting on a floral shirt and blue serge trousers. Once he glanced at himself in the full-length mirror and thought that he was losing weight, but when he buttoned up his trousers he found them tight. Looking at himself dressed he felt unsatisfied. There was no one detail that stood out as bad. It was more a desire to improve them all. Before he left the room he checked to see if he had the address and the street map. Peter had told him he wouldn't need a map—if he got off the bus at the bowling club and walked up the hill, he couldn't miss the house with the flowering jacaranda tree. Peter would be waiting. He had sounded a little nervous on the phone, but that had been the trend, they were all a bit anxious and, of course, lonely.

The place where he had breakfast, a health food bar, was already full of tourists talking loudly and laughing. A few were quite red. A white skin from a cool climate suddenly meets the strong tropical sun, little suspecting its strength. They looked cooked and painful, an appearance usually reserved for Europeans. Two men were talking in French. Then he recognised a German accent. He closed his eyes and listened. The voice was close to that of a friend in Sydney, Hans. The laugh was identical.

It was Hans who had put the idea into his head. 'You need contacts,' Hans would say. 'This country is a big place. Hitchhike in Europe, you get rides short distance. For longer lift they stop every half hour for break. The first lift I get in Australia, the driver keep driving, never stop for hours. I say, 'I got to piss.' So he stop on the road. I say 'Where is the toilet?' He laughed. We get out. We both piss on side of road. When we get back in the car he says to me, 'You got a big cock.' Hans would always laugh at this point. A loud laugh, slightly mechanical, like it had been triggered off by the word 'cock'.

When he heard that Carlos planned to travel around Australia, Hans had suggested that he put an ad in one of the gay newspapers. They sat up one night composing it. 'You need to describe yourself,' said Hans, his Biro gripped tightly in his hand, waiting for the words to come.

Carlos thought about a description—middle aged, male, slightly fat and balding, the hair greying. Not very alluring, yet his smile was youthful and hinted at a charm that carried him through hard times. There was a toughness in the face that marked him as a survivor. 'Good looking,' said Carlos, with a giggle.

'Masculine, yah, they do not like effeminate types here.'

'Masculine ethnic from the Dominican Republic.'

'They do not know the Dominican Republic here. They

never hear of Wuppertale either. German Hans, yes. Big cock, yes.' The laugh again. It was as if they were describing another and Carlos' confidence grew.

MAN FROM THE CARIBBEAN, TRAVELLING AROUND AUSTRALIA, SEEKS DALLIANCE ALONG THE WAY. ALL TOWNS CONSIDERED. NO CHICKEN.

'Dalliance' was not a word either man would normally have used, but as it was often used in the other ads, they went with that.

Carlos was away a few months, picking fruit at Young. It was a way of making money, although the work was hard. He lost weight in the process and Hans complimented him on his health appearance when he reappeared in Sydney, eager to taste again the fleshy delights only a large city can offer. Hans handed him a large bundle of letters.

'All this mail for me?' asked Carlos. Usually there were only a few letters—his sister in Miami, a few friends in Los Angeles, occasionally some postcards from people he had met on his travels, but these correspondences seldom lasted more than a year. His mother had died five years before but while she was alive she had faithfully corresponded twice every month. Sometimes the letters he received had been readdressed three times. Then he remembered the ad he and Hans had put in the magazine.

He took the letters to his room, read each one several times, then put them in careful piles. In one pile he put the 'mad' ones. He could not quite make any sense of these. In some even the English was incomprehensible. One went on for pages about the life of the writer, entirely missing the point of the assignation. Another brought up the subject of God and repentance, offering salvation for the sinner. He put in this pile of rejects a letter from a 15-year-old boy who was just coming out. Carlos had stated in the ad that he did not want young boys but this person had not understood the meaning of 'no chicken'.

Next there was the sensible pile, where the writers gave brief accounts of their hopes for him and the descriptions on themselves. He was relieved that most letters fitted into this pile. Then there were the fetishists for whom the word 'Caribbean' had conjured up visions of chocolate skin, abandoned passion and steamy sex on tropical nights. Without exception they all wanted to know the size of his cock. Their imagination had not stopped here. They went on to indulge their own fantasies: spanking, submission, master and slave, bondage. One had a desire to be kidnapped and taken to a hotel room in handcuffs. One letter had a drawing of a large, erect penis across the top of the page. The outline was bold and accurately drawn but the shading, though meticulous, was not realistic.

The last pile he looked at the most: those who sent photos of themselves. Some had photos taken in studios: these photos were well lit, with highlights on the cheeks and hair, and the subjects' smiling teeth in focus. Two people were part-time actors, another a radiographer who worked with cameras. Most of the other photos were not in focus, nor did they flatter the sitters, who stared out from living rooms, backyards and bedrooms, some in states of undress, others completely nude, all with an expectant look on their faces. Do you like me?

Carlos put all the letters into a box and although he talked about them to Hans he never let Hans read them. (Later this was to cause a rift between them, Hans accusing him of being ungrateful.) The next day he went to a service station and bought a map of Australia.

After breakfast, he checked again to see if he still had the address in his pocket, then he dawdled in the shopping centres, shopping for nothing in particular. At one place they had shiny didgeridoos stacked out in the front and at a travel agency there were rows of pamphlets describing diving and rafting trips. In a clothes shop which displayed cowboy outfits in the front window, he decided he wanted to change his appearance. He looked too naively colourful, as if he had just come off some tourist cruise from Hawaii— all he lacked was a lai of frangipani around his neck. He tried on boots and checked western shirts, but they didn't feel right. He ended up buying black working jeans and a shiny black shirt that had white stitching around the pockets, and triangular metal clasps at the tips of the collar. He also bought a leather thong with matching silver metal tips to tie around his neck. It was an attempt to look masculine although it didn't quite come off—something about his overall shape. At least he had changed to dark clothes. That was a concession to the expectations of many who had answered his ad. They had assumed that a 'man from the Caribbean' would be a big black stud.

On the bus he saw an old woman with a scarf and thought of Delores del Miguel. When he lived in Los Angeles, Carlos had been to her sex workshops. Her method of increasing potency, pleasure and potential was drawn from new age ideas that abounded in the area, techniques of increasing self esteem and assertiveness and, of course, the classic of erotica, the Kama Sutra. At times, to increase his potential, Delores would have him imitate animals. She had him purring like a snow leopard or squealing like a pig. Her great talent was to bring her customers in touch with their inner sexual selves. He remembered her—small, dark, wrinkled, a map of hardship etched into her face, yet her expression shone with kindness and positivity. She was not good looking and she was old, but she exuded a kittenish sexuality. 'All humans, no matter how they look, have sexual potential,' she would say. Turning to Carlos, as if he needed more encouragement, she would add, 'Remember, Carlos, there is always hope in this world.'

The bowling station came into view. Carlos got off the bus and looked up the hill. The street was piled with furniture and boxes of rubbish. There was some sort of communal throw out—books spilled onto grassy lawns, kitchenware dribbled into the gutter and clothes trailed out of empty chests and cartons. When he was halfway up the hill, he realised that the shirt was a mistake. It absorbed the heat of the sun and became very hot. He picked up a magazine from a box and fanned himself.

The house was exactly as Peter said it would be. A timber house with double hung windows and a verandah at the front. A large jacaranda tree shaded it in part. On either side of the front path a bed of zinnias had been planted—cheerful, colourful flowers. The house had a homely look. He expected to smell a barbecue and the aroma of home-baked apple pie.

Carlos arranged himself at the door, tucking in his shirt, wiping the sweat off his face with a handkerchief. Then he rang the doorbell. He still had the magazine in his hand, so he fanned himself once more, then wondered what to do with it. A black cat slept on a bench at the end of the veranda. He was going to leave the magazine on the bench when he looked at the cover and saw it was a pornographic magazine, *Screw*. A large-breasted woman smiled invitingly at him. He had picked this up quite innocently from the carton, thinking it was a *Women's Weekly* or something. He couldn't leave it on the bench nor did he want to meet Peter while holding it. He considered whether he should go back and put it in the box where he found it, but that seemed silly. The front door opened.

A tall, dark-haired woman in a blue dress and a white

feather boa looked at him from behind the door. Carlos hesitated, wondering if he had make a mistake, if he had come to the right place. 'Is Peter in?' he asked. There was a moment of awkwardness where neither party could resolve this question and it hung there, like the riddle of the Sphinx. An incorrect answer might shatter the assignation. Carlos reached to his pocket to check the address and at the same time the woman opened the door a little wider. 'Do come in,' she smiled. He walked in. The woman gave an immense sigh of relief, as if the first hurdle had been overcome, and her expression changed from tension to a conspirational intimacy. 'Thank goodness you've arrived.' The deep register of the voice alerted Carlos. Red lipstick and the pale makeup covered the dark stubble. The woman was a man. The door closed behind him.

Carlos entered the living room which was large and neatly decorated with a loungesuite, a coffee table, several shelves of books and a sideboard which incorporated a TV set. Into this suburban setting, the woman whirled. With a flourish of the boa she indicated a seat. 'Do sit down.' Carlos sat stiffly on the couch while the woman arranged herself opposite in a single armchair in the sprawling manner of a cat, although the angles she made were awkward. 'Call me Desiree.' She smiled expansively.

Carlos smiled wanly and tucked the magazine into the side of the chair. Because he could not think of any compliment for Desiree's appearance he commented on the weather. 'It's nice and cool in here.'

'It's cool in summer because of the big jacaranda tree, but it loses its leaves in winter and we get lovely warm sun.' With her hands, Desiree indicated the beautiful sunlight streaming in through the window. The feather boa gave a fluttering effect to her poetic statement, then she became more reflective and serious. 'But you should be used to the warm weather, isn't the Caribbean tropical?

'It is, but I haven't lived there for a long time. I don't remember it being as hot as the north of Australia. There was always a sea breeze where we lived.'

'Yes, it's a different kind of heat here.'

'I'm getting used to it.'

'Yes, you always can acclimatise.'

'I've had cold showers every day.'

Cold showers. It was a chance to bring up the subject of sex.

In her dreams Desiree had imagined Carlos to be much taller, broader shouldered, blacker, with heavy forearms and thick lips. The model of her fantasies had been the cover to a paperback, *Mandingo*, which she had read as her alter ego, Peter. The book had not satisfied her, but it had sharpened a fantasy of her own, in which a large, black man appeared from nowhere, perhaps a fugitive from the law, needing help from her. In some way, he was in her power, depending on her. She cleverly deceived the pursuing police and sent them away. When she and the black man, whose shirt was torn to reveal powerful pecs and well-defined abdomens, were alone he was overcome by a fierce desire for her. She protested at first, but so strong was his passion, she gave in. He ripped the evening gown from her (always she was in a full frock from the first half of *Gone with the Wind*), then the black stud would penetrate her, crushing her with his great weight and powerful thrusts.

But Carlos, slumped on the couch, was none of the things of her fantasy. He was slightly pot bellied, coffee coloured, and he had a moustache which reminded her of a character she had seen in an American high school movie who played the supporting role of a janitor. He was starting to sweat, the perspiration staining his armpits. She had a desire to mop his brow with a handkerchief, but she had none, so instead she offered him a drink.

'What would you like to drink?'

'What have you got? Something cool.'

'A mint dewlip?' She fluttered her eyelashes. 'Then there's always beer.'

'A beer would be nice.'

He had started drinking beer since he was in Australia, as a way of integrating. He fitted into people's expectations. His favourite drink was rum but he thought a request for rum could be complicated and the situation was complicated enough.

While Desiree was in the kitchen Carlos looked around at the decorations in the room. Local scenes in oils hung around the room, along with a few framed posters—a Paris Opera production of *The Magic Flute* and a local production of *The Importance of Being Earnest*. Someone in the house collected matching cups and saucers with polka-dotted designs and tall cocktail glasses in different-coloured glass from the fifties. On the TV set stood photos of a family group. A dark-haired man, who was obviously Desiree out of drag, stood next to a woman with short-cropped hair, and a young girl who was presumably their daughter, held a cat. Children's books and a child's drawings taped to the wall indicated the presence of a child.

Desiree came brightly into the room with a tray made of patchwork wood on which sat a glass of beer and a cocktail glass of clear liquid. She sat on the couch next to Carlos and pulled up a small table with a laminex top. She gave him the glass of beer with a smile and daintily took the cocktail glass for herself and put the tray on the side-table.

'We were out of mint, so I made myself a gin and tonic.'

'Cheers,' said Carlos, lifting his glass. 'To us.'

It was a gallant gesture, and Desiree twittered in appreciation. They clicked glasses and took deep swallows.

'Nice beer,' said Carlos, although he had not yet developed a taste for beer and really couldn't tell one from the other.

'It's Fourex, a Queensland beer. They make it in Brisbane. You come from Sydney, don't you?' asked Desiree.

'Sydney is my base. I've been travelling around Australia.'

'Sydney is a wild place. Do you spend much time in Oxford Street?'

'I have been to Oxford Street but I don't spend much time in bars.'

'Then what do you like to do? How does Carlos get his fun?'

It was an invitation and he boldly put his hand on her thigh. She tittered.

'Naughty boy,' she said coyly and pushed his hand away.

There was a long pause where she regretted her impulsive response and feared that she had crushed his desire too soon.

Carlos looked around the room and began a new conversation.

'Who did the paintings?' he asked.

'Oh, just a friend.' It was actually a friend of Peter's wife but it was too complicated to explain. It seemed a mistake to have all this happening in the living room. There was too much around to remind her of her other life. It was easier in a bar to have an identity away from the mundane world. It had been a mistake to bring him here. They should have met at a bar at night. But she had already rejected that possibility. First, she would have had to make some excuse to get out of the house. And the one bar they could have gone to only opened on Saturday night. Her appearance there would have been public, totally open to gossip. No it was not a possibility. Better to dim the lights and blot out the mundane world.

'It's too bright. A girl should not be subjected to this harsh tropic light. It dries the skin.'

Desiree got up from the couch and pulled down the blinds and drew the curtains across the french doors opening onto the verandah. She did not close the doors or the windows, so occasionally the wind would lift the curtain and a soft light would momentarily flood the room. While she was up she took the tray.

'I'll just top us up.' She gave a little squint at the naughtiness of her suggestion, then she went back to the kitchen.

Carlos watched her leave the room. He would have liked Desiree as a man. He could see, beneath the too-thick makeup, the too-red lipstick, Peter's dark good looks, the bedroom eyes, the sensuous mouth and the slim body. All the drag, frankly got in the way. Carlos had not had a lot of experience with women, yet he found here, in Australia, that they fell into set roles. (Desiree was the desirable woman, and it was up to him, the man from the Caribbean, to make the move.) Everything was exaggerated. He felt they were in a soap opera and the playing of their parts, already written, would lead to an inevitable ending—sex. Well, that was the subplot when he first wrote the ad. They both understood that.

Desiree brought in the tray with an opened bottle of beer, gin and tonic bottles and the glasses, already full.

'Saves me the trouble,' she said apologetically, referring to the bottles on the tray, as if she had let her standards slip.

As if to reinforce this, she sat closer to him on the couch and they each drank deeply from their glasses. The

room now seemed cool and dark and the assorted paraphernalia seemed hidden from view. Occasionally the breeze
blew open the curtain but it was not a distraction and she
was able to put these reminders of domestic life out of her
mind.

'The light is much kinder now, that's the trouble with
the day.'

'The light in Port of Spain is bright like this, but in the
house where I grew up the windows were small and the
interior was dark. I remember as a boy I'd run out of the
house and I'd be blinded by the light in the street.'

It seemed to her a terrifying image—a place so bright
there was nowhere to hide.

'Do you remember that scene from *Streetcar* where Carl
Malden and Blanche are in the room together? He'd just
agreed to marry her. She'd told him she was a young thing.
There was some deception involved but it was not her fault.
He was a cruel man and he forced her head under the naked
light bulb to see her face. He saw that she was old. She
never recovered from that.'

She involuntarily sighed. It was her favourite moment
of all her favourite movies. The mere thought of it caused
her to feel despondent. She regretted she had steered the
conversation towards tragedy when really she was better
being bright and vivacious.

Although he had not seen the movie, Carlos was nev-
ertheless a kind man and he responded to her vulnerability.
It gave him a chance to put his arm around her and draw
her closer. This time she did not push him away. She melted
into his arm. He felt bolder and began to feel her shoulder
which was slender though firm, and his hand began to undo
the front of her dress. She wore a padded brassiere which
he caressed and squeezed and she gave a positive response
to this. He continued, slightly amazed that this would excite

her since all he felt was the rough seams of the brassiere and the spongy rubber of the padding. Then he slipped his hand underneath, which was quite easy since the brassiere had become loose, and felt large male nipples and in the dish of the chest a patch of soft hair, which he found exciting. He had found a man beneath the makeup. Encouraged, he kissed her on the mouth. The lipstick was thick and it had a sticky texture but soon they were devouring each other, eating the lipstick that smeared their faces. The makeup was rubbing off and Carlos felt increased desire at the stubble of her chin.

It was here that Desiree felt an anticipation of dissatisfaction. Having done all the work—for it was she who could make the bright chatter, who could fill those awkward silences, who had the confidence to take control, who could be bold and make advances, who opened the fly of Carlos as he half lay on the couch in the semi-darkened room and took his cock into her mouth (yes, it was Desiree who did all this, Desiree, the sex slave of Peter)—she knew, at the moment of her triumph, that Peter would discard her and take all this pleasure for himself.

As Desiree performed the torrid fellatio, Carlos remembered the teaching of Delores del Miguel and he began to squirm and purr like a snow leopard and then to yelp like a dog.

Desiree had been disappointed that his cock had not been bigger, but as he pumped it into her mouth, alternatively purring and yelping, a feeling of ecstasy came over her and she felt her own cock stiffen in her pantyhose and she knew her femininity was disappearing and her alter ego, Peter, was taking control.

Carlos commanded her in an authoritative tone (another manifestation of the del Miguel technique) to lie on her back and it was in this position that he penetrated her. His cock in her hurt slightly although he was not rough and the sensation was somewhere between pleasure and pain. It was nothing like she had imagined from the pictures on the covers of the romantic novels she devoured. She tried, as an act of will, to visualise a favourite scene while this rather sweaty act was performed, with its unforeseen juices dribbling onto the couch. She had very little of the props of identity left—the smeared lipstick the last remaining vestige on which to cling. Her clothes were scattered around the room and the wig had somehow fallen between cushions. Desiree was losing herself to Peter who was moaning and whimpering in an uncontrolled way. His was the greater experience. When he called out as if from a dream, 'Dad. Dad. Don't do it,' she knew she was gone.

They wiped off the sticky cum and recovered their breaths. A shaft of sunlight managed to avoid the branches of the jacaranda tree, penetrate the louvres of the verandah and find the only gap in the drawn curtain through which to cast a small bright spot on the floor. Movement in the branches outside caused the spot to waver in its intensity so it had the appearance of a living thing, a chameleon-like creature changing its appearance rapidly, wilfully, yet doomed to disappear with the movement of the planets.

'It was my father,' said Peter. 'He caught me at my mother's sewing machine. I was just sewing a shirt. All his disappointments in me were manifested when he saw me there. All his dreams for me were shattered. He pushed the sewing machine off the table, onto the floor. He ripped up the shirt and then he hit me. "No son of mine going to be a nancy boy," he said.'

Yet Carlos could not answer for he, too, was lost in his own thoughts, of escapades and physical hurts he had experienced as a boy trying to escape the city of Santo Domingo, surviving as an illegal immigrant in Los Angeles and, of course, the fateful and fortuitous meeting with Delores del Miguel.

Though both were lost in their own world there was a physical contact between them as Carlos slumped beside Peter and Peter's arm fell over his chest. Already sweat was forming from the contact of the flesh and it would take only a small heave to break it. They both knew that they would go their separate ways. Yet there was a bond they would not lose. They were like some bird enthusiasts who had travelled a long way to see a rare bird at a distant mountain. The bird may not have been spectacular in any way, but it had meant something to each of them, an experience they would always keep, yet would find difficult to describe to others.

Then came a sound which had the effect of a speeding car, careering out of control across the low gutter, splintering the white-painted posts of the wire fence, churning the plot of zinnias, throwing up brightly coloured petals like confetti in the wind, before smashing into the front of the house. A key turning in the lock of the door.

Carlos felt Peter's arm stiffen. Peter sat up. Carlos heard the door open and the sound of footsteps in the corridor. The sound seemed slowly to seep around the door into the room at the speed of water spreading from an overflowing tap. Peter stood and picked up his wig. In the doorway there appeared a purple and white petal, a bud, a green stem, a bunch of blooms carried by a woman with short hair, wearing a floral blouse and loose cream shorts. In her other hand she carried a plastic bag of groceries. She looked into the room but did not stop. Peter said, 'Shit,' and slunk out of the room carrying a few, but certainly not all, of his garments.

As Carlos dressed he listened to the sound of the woman unpacking the groceries in the kitchen. Clunk. The fridge door opened, the crisper was pulled out. Caloomp caloomp, carrots were poured in. Tins of peaches were put on shelves. The pottery lid of the bread bin closed. After he dressed, Carlos was presented with a choice of whether he should just leave or stay. To leave seemed shabby, he had deceived no one. He had been in situations like this before and though they were certainly awkward, he had found them unpredictable rather than dangerous. Hans had told him of situations which he had been in. 'They will attack each other first. Whatever you do, don't take sides.' Carlos resolutely sat on the couch, resolving to stay and resisting an impulse not to pick up the scattered clothes.

The woman came into the room, acknowledged Carlos' presence with a glance and went over to a shelf and picked up a large green vase.

'I need this,' she said. 'This is the only vase which will hold waterlilies. They flop over the side. Christine gave me a bunch. They've got a dam.'

Carlos noted her haircut, the short trousers, her broad shoulders and flat breasts. She's like a good-looking young man, he thought. That's why he probably married her in the first place, she reminded him of a boy.

'Where's Peter?' she said, looking at Carlos.

He felt ridiculous in his black shirt, sweating, and for the first time in the house, he felt overweight.

'He's gone to change,' he answered.

'Oh,' she said. She went to leave, but paused.

'Would you like tea?' she asked.

Carlos nodded. 'Thank you.'

Then, as if registering his dripping condition, she added considerately, 'Or perhaps you'd like a cool drink?'

'Tea will be fine,' he said.

They had found a common subject, and were busily talking

about the advantages and disadvantages of organic gardening. Already on their second cup of tea when Peter entered the room, dressed in a white shirt and cream trousers, his hair still wet from the shower, as if he had just come back from a game of tennis.

He smiled. 'You have met? Carol, my wife, Carlos . . .' How would he describe their relationship? My friend, my most recent one-night stand?

'We've met,' Carol said dryly. And there was a short silence.

'There could be storm, it's hot enough,' said Peter, pouring himself a cup.

'There are aren't any clouds, though the garden could do with a drink,' Carol said thoughtfully.

'It's not the wet season yet, is it?' Carlos asked. 'Everyone warned me not to come here in the wet season.'

'No, that doesn't start till January or February, and if we're lucky we'll get a good cyclone,' Peter said expansively, laughing a little at his own joke.

'Is a cyclone like a tornado?' Carlos asked.

'No, it's a different thing,' said Carol.

'No, it's the same, it's just a different name. The Americans call it a tornado,' said Peter knowingly.

'It's not,' said Carol. 'A tornado is like a big whirlwind whereas a cyclone is like a strong wind.'

'A cyclone is like a whirlwind too, haven't you seen the weather patterns of cloud? It's circular.'

'But a tornado has a centre, it's like a long funnel stretching from the land to the clouds, and it picks up things.'

'It's the same with a cyclone. The cyclone has a centre. Haven't you heard of the eye of the cyclone?' He had become petulant.

Carol turned to Carlos. 'Have you even been in a tornado?'

'No,' he replied, 'but I've seen them on the television.'

'They are like long funnels, aren't they?'

He was being dragged into the tornado. He remembered the story of an old cow that had been sucked up in the spout, spun in the air for about a mile, deposited on the roof of a house, and still, miraculously, survived.

'Yes,' he answered.

He regretted that he had said that. He should have been noncommittal. He should have said, 'I believe so,' or, 'I don't remember.' That would have been better than 'yes', because now he had taken sides. The image came to him of Hans shaking his head, muttering, 'You dumb prick, what did I tell you? Ya.'

'See,' said Carol, now that she had the backing of a second opinion to support her, 'I know what I'm talking about, I teach it to the children.'

'So that makes you some sort of know-all,' said Peter. He had turned sour. 'Well, let me tell you, what they teach isn't always right. What they teach to children isn't necessarily true.'

'I've never taught a child anything that I didn't believe was true,' said Carol.

There was a silence, as if they had been though this same argument before and reached the same, inevitable conclusion which was always unsatisfactory to both. Each was obviously reluctant to go through the motions again.

'Would you like some more tea, Carlos?' asked Carol, sweetly.

Carlos shook his head. He had had enough.

Peter remained in a sulky mood.

'I should be getting back to my hotel.'

'Where are you staying?'

'At the Esplanade.'

'Oh, that's nice there.'

'Don't go,' said Peter.

'Oh, I must get back,' said Carlos, trying to think of a pressing reason.

'You could stay for dinner,' said Peter, brightening up, throwing off his sombre mood, proving he could be good company. 'I make a very nice pasta, from real eggs. I make the noodle myself.'

'I've already arranged to have dinner, I'm sorry,' said Carlos firmly.

'I'm sure you've got many contacts in this town,' said Peter without malice.

It was true. Carlos had another appointment tomorrow, but nothing tonight. He was looking forward to a quiet meal in a Spanish restaurant where a guitarist played tunes he knew. He wanted to get out of this suburban house, with its tensions and accusations.

'I've got this great bottle of Henschke red we could open.'

'I should be going,' said Carlos firmly.

'It's still early. What are you doing till seven?' Peter insisted.

'For goodness sake Peter, Carlos wants to go,' said Carol. There was a silence. Peter pouted.

'Angela will be coming home from school soon,' said Carol.

'So what? Do we have to kick Carlos out? Is everything so irregular? Do we have to bring out Tupperware and Bibles to show we are normal?'

Carol turned sharply to Carlos. 'You're not the first one, there have been others.'

Whereas she had seemed quite cool and rational before, her voice now had a brittle edge and Carlos knew a little psychodrama was about to be played out. It was the sort of thing Delores encouraged among couples, but in the safer environment of her studio. 'We will get down to the source of things,' Delores would say.

Carol turned to Peter. 'You made a complete fool of yourself at that party after the play. You looked so bad with that wig, with your shirt tied up. Malcolm was stupid too.'

Peter, reminded of a party after a play by the local dramatic society, assumed a dramatic stance. 'Malcolm is a great actor, he has talent. He is a beautiful man. We never in all those years had an Ernest like him. And he can sing. What a voice.'

'Malcolm can sing, to be sure. But you both looked ridiculous, gyrating on that stage, singing that song.'

Peter began to sing, 'I go to Rio'. He gave pelvic thrusts. He did look slightly ridiculous, but engaging as well. He turned to Carlos. 'You should have heard the applause. They loved us. They loved us. They wanted an encore.'

Carol, reminded of a part of the story she had chosen to forget, started to pick up the remaining clothes that had been tossed around the room.

'You don't have to get rid of everything,' said Peter. He grabbed the brassiere from Carol's arm and flung it across the room. Carol, keeping her head down, continued to search for bits of clothes.

A stiletto shoe had lodged under the couch and Carol tugged at it. Peter went over and tugged at the shoe as well. The shoe became dislodged and they both held it. They fought over the shoe like two dogs over a bone. 'Give me that shoe. It belongs to me.' Peter had the shoe but the voice was Desiree's. 'It was given to me by an admirer. A rich admirer from London.'

Somehow it was as if another person was in the room. Someone with a totally different case history, whose reason for wanting the shoe was entirely different from either Peter's or Carol's.

Both Carol and Carlos stared at this person standing there, holding the shoe. It was Desiree who stared back at them defiantly. For a moment she glowered at them magnificently, but this Desiree, rather like a general without an army, did not have her props. In the absence of frocks, wigs and makeup she began to crumble before their eyes. Desiree became helpless, vulnerable, lost and childlike. It was a transformation similar to one that Carlos had seen in a movie when a vampire, confronted by the light of day, began to dry up and corrode—the flesh crumbling like fine sand from the bones. Peter began to cry and slumped into a chair like a child who had been hit. Carol immediately went over to him and held him. He clung to her. The sobbing increased then eased. He said he was sorry he was such a slut but he couldn't help himself. She forgave him. They made up as if Carlos wasn't even there. Carlos had the feeling he was watching a film.

'I hope I didn't cause you any trouble,' Carlos said to Carol at the front door as he was leaving.

'No,' said Carol, 'I'm used to these things.'

'Goodbye,' Carlos said to Peter, shaking his hand. 'You have my address in Sydney if you want to write.'

'Goodbye,' said Peter, brightly. He had completely recovered, was playing the part of the charming host. 'Sorry you couldn't stay for dinner.'

The door closed. Carlos remembered the pornographic magazine he had left tucked in the corner of the couch but he did not got back.

As he walked to the front gate, he saw a young girl, about nine years old, running down the street. She carried a long silky scarf which trailed behind her as she ran. The colours were bright but not gaudy. A gold thread running through the fabric caught the light. They met at the gate.

'Have you been visiting us?' asked the girl.

'Yes, we had tea,' said Carlos lightly, as if he had participated in a gentle suburban ritual that had been performed many times in that town.

'Where did you get that?' Carlos asked of the scarf.

'They've got lots of tat in the street. There's been a throw out. I found it. It's nice, isn't it? It's for my Dad, he likes to dress up.'

She ran inside.

The man from the Caribbean watched the bright scarf shimmer in the sunlight. He thought of the words of Delores del Miguel, 'Carlos, there is always hope in this world.' Then he walked on.

BUTCHERS APRONS

ALANA VALENTINE

Crown had been invited to an offal-eating afternoon tea. At least she thought that they were going to eat offal. Janet had said 'an offal party' and since Janet struck her as fairly balanced person, Crown dismissed thoughts of bizarre cult rituals and rationalized the event as an exercise in boosting the womens' iron intake. She wondered why Janet had invited her, since she had never expressed any particular passion for offal. But, Crown thought, people often ask you to do things with them for their own selfish reasons. Crown tried to remember what offal she had ever swallowed. She had regularly eaten chicken livers several years ago, served with cream and mushrooms. But now she preferred semi-sweet cakes. On special occasions she liked to eat crab marinated with chilli followed by coffee-flavoured mousse. Crown wondered if it was Janet's birthday. If she had known she would have bought her a wooden animal with moveable joints.

Janet had told her that there would be four other women coming over for the party. No names had been mentioned when Janet had invited her. It occurred to Crown that one of the guests may have recently been to a funeral. It used to be that a person's vanity was the easiest thing to access in conversation but these days Crown found that grief was the fast track to intimacy. Unfortunately Crown intensely disliked consoling people, though she herself loved to be consoled. She liked to sit with other people, strangers, and have them say, 'I'm sure everything is going to be all right.' She particularly enjoyed it when they couldn't possibly know whether it would be all right or not. The absurdity of it delighted her. Which was why she disliked consoling people herself, knowing as she did that terrible things do happen all the time.

The house Janet lived in was built from white-painted wooden slats, with a concreted verandah. In the front garden white jonquils bloomed in a jagged row, their frilly little flowers looking impossibly vulnerable. Crown knocked on the front door and watched through the glass slats as a figure moved toward her. But she was mistaken. No foot-steps accompanied the apparition. She knocked again and this time trusted her ears rather than her eyes that someone was coming.

Janet showed Crown into the lounge room where the other women were already seated around a wooden table. The women smiled at her and invited her to sit in a seat with a pale green cushion on it. All the women were dressed in clean white coats and were wearing blue and white striped butchers aprons. It gave the effect of walking into a country newsagency where all the shop assistants wear matching clothes. Janet introduced Crown to the other women and they smiled again, warmly and welcomingly. No one said a sulky 'hello' or an aggressive 'yes' that indicated Crown had forgotten meeting them once before. Janet handed Crown a coat and apron and asked her if she would like to go and get changed into it while they went and got the offal.

Crown went into the bedroom and slipped off her zip-up top. She was going to leave her jeans on and the cotton spencer that kept in the heat. The room smelt of rose oil and the clothes of the other women hung on a hat rack at the base of the bed. There were coats folded over a cane chair that was set in the corner where the skirting board met the floor. Crown pulled on the butcher's uniform and admired its white stiffness. She wrapped the apron around her and wove the strings back and forth around her waist, strapping herself into the stripes and knotting the ties in a secure fix.

When she went back into the lounge room there were six enamel dishes on the table with single raw body parts in them. There was a sheep's heart and a cow's stomach lining and a chicken's liver and brains and intestine and kidney. Two of the women were drinking red wine and the others had glasses of water. Janet smiled at Crown and asked if she had trouble getting here what with the buses refusing to take standing passengers. No, she said, she caught the train and walked here. She'd get a taxi home. One of the other women (who Janet has introduced as Lillee) suggested that they should begin.

Lillee turned to Crown and asked her would she like to go first. No, she would not like to go first. Crown looked at them all and demurred. She sat straightening her apron while they took in her heavy, freckled arms, beautiful brown eyes and shiny straight hair. Crown looked around the table at the anticipation in the faces of the other women and said she would just like to watch first. She would just like to watch, she said in the tone one reserves for entering clothes shops and shooing off the assistant by saying you are 'just looking, thanks'.

Janet wondered about her decision to invite Crown. She had done so because she was impressed by Crown's height. Tall people need almost do nothing else in their lives than be physically above average, as far as Janet was concerned. Since nothing could diminish the power of bodily extension,

Janet found it fascinating that such people should struggle or be insecure in any other way. As she looked at Crown in the butcher's apron that she had provided, Janet also admitted to herself that she had invited Crown because she was scared of having an affair with her. Not that Crown had offered, or that Janet would take up the offer if she did. Janet simply lived in continual fear of changing herself by having an affair with someone. Unconsciously she distrusted her own ability to get out of situations that she didn't like once she was in them.

The woman who had been introduced as Meredith said, 'Why don't I begin then?' She pulled one of the enamel plates towards her—Crown thought it held the liver—and picked it up with her left hand. The liver dripped. Meredith was a blonde, curly-haired woman with soft, slightly red cheeks and clear-rimmed glasses. She looked like she could probably sing very well, with a full, operatic voice. With a shock Crown saw her take the liver and hold it above her left shoulder where it leaked in small lines down the side of her white top as she spoke.

'I remember in the past when I was young, maybe five or six, and our family were living in a stinking back lane above a shop. The only way into the flat was through the corrugated iron back fence which had a hole cut into it and a hinged wooden door attached to it with rusting bolts. There was a woman who lived downstairs who had cats, their piss choking all the life from the assortment of harrowed-looking plants that served as some sort of garden for the tenants' children. My brother and I used to go down there and talk to her, making abusive comments to her that we knew she wouldn't repeat to our mother. One day we found kittens and we went shouting to tell her, carrying the small bundles into her kitchen, our eyes gleaming with delight at the mewing scrawniness of the little cats.

'The woman shook her head and put the plug in the sink. When it was half full of warm water she took one of the kittens from us and without further comment held its head under the water until it drowned. She asked me if I would like to help her with the next one and indicated that I should bring the two cats I had to her. I held tightly on to the neck of the kitten in my right hand and she thrust it under the water. As the animal struggled for its life, the kitten in the other hand began to squirm. There was such a delight in feeling that I, a child, had the strength to hold down a struggling life till I could feel the fighting get weaker and my fingers loosened their grip. I pushed the kitten's head under for some time longer and then pulled it from the sink, its damp fur dripping as I carried it to the plastic bag where the old woman had placed the other dead kitten. It was my brother's turn.'

Meredith finished her story and looked down at the table. She replaced the liver into the enamel dish in front of her, her right hand holding it there. She wiped her other hand onto the front of her white apron, the messy patch making a contrast to the lines of thin drips which were still wet. Crown thought that what was required of her was a story of past guilt, a sort of opportunity to relieve regrets that were in some way connected to one of the internal organs on the table. She raked through her catalogue of remembered traumas.

'I will go next,' said a woman whose breasts were straining at the fit of the white, high-collared butcher's shirt. She pulled towards her the slice of tripe, which was clean and almost dry in comparison to the bloodiness of the other pieces of offal. She picked the piece of white flesh up and then bought it slapping down onto the table. She did so as though she were beating mats on some sunny balcony, trying to dislodge accumulations of lint or dust. But the piece did not yield any flying particles, nor even a spray of any clinging juices.

'I remember when I was eleven and I was still sharing a bedroom with my 7-year-old cousin. I used to make her lick my vagina at night. She would have to go under the sheets and blankets so that no one would see her if they came in. One night my uncle did come in and my cousin was between my legs under the bedclothes. My uncle pulled the sheets off and saw my cousin and slapped her hard on the face and told her to get to the bathroom and wash her face.

'He had on a beaded belt with FIJI on it in blue and red and white beads and he told me to turn over while he took off his belt. I could hear the soft whoosh of the leather as he whipped it out of its place. Then he started to belt me and he was screaming at me that I was a little slut that I was a no good slut that I was a filthy little bitch and he was hitting me with the belt and he was hitting me so hard that the belt broke and all the beads went all over the bed. I turned around and just saw my little cousin standing at the door, her hand up to her mouth to stop her screaming out, and my uncle saw her, too, and he threw the end of the belt on the bed and slammed the door after him as he left.'

The woman, whose name Crown did not remember, was slapping herself with the piece of tripe, not with great force, more like one might swat oneself with a plastic flyswat if bothered by summer insects. The offal left small damp patches on her butcher's apron which were slightly yellow but without blood. Crown thought that perhaps she was not required to be guilty for something; perhaps they were trying to look back and find someone else to blame. Crown tried to think of a malicious event which she could lose herself in. The woman was looking up now and laughing, not giggling or enjoying herself, but looking suddenly self-conscious and laughing so that the others laughed with her and looked quizzically at the remaining dishes.

None of the women were wearing jewellery or other adornments, and Crown realised that only Janet wore the small bow-tie sometimes associated with butchers. A tall thin woman now stood. She was wearing a leather knife-holster but there were no knives in it. She reached into the centre of the table and pulled the intestine towards her. 'Phew, it stinks,' she said to the gathering. Meredith offered to go and wash it for her. But the woman (whose name was Leonie) spat a little into the bowl and rubbed the slimy intestine around in it.

'I remember when I was fourteen, at agriculture camp, and all the campers were very excited because that day we were going to see a cow being dissected. We all gathered in a field and the farmer had a slit cow hanging on a hook in the back of a utility truck. The farmer and the cow were on a stage provided by the tray of the truck. The farmer pulled aside the flap of the ruptured cow and pulled out various internal organs to show us where and what they were. Then he pulled out the intestine and told one of the boys in the audience to see how far he could run down the road with it.

'The boy jumped up onto the truck and grabbed the end of the organ and then jumped off and ran down the dirt track, the intestine stretching for what seemed like a city block. Everyone was laughing and awed by the length of the cow's intestine. The intestine, now covered in dirt, was brought back to the truck, looped like rope from a docking ferry. The cow continued to hang suspended, a hook through its throat, and its innards hanging out like tentacles from a giant jellyfish. The boy who had run with the intestine was trying to stuff the intestine back into the cow when suddenly the farmer came up behind him and, with a firm push, shoved the boy's head inside the animal's gut. The boy struggled as the farmer laughed and looked out to the crowd of children for adulation. Finally he released the boy's neck and the child pulled back, his face glazed with bloody chunks and his eyes rolling in terror. The crowd clapped as the boys scraped the innards out of his nose and mouth.'

Now it was Crown's turn. She began to panic that she would not have something horrible and moving to contribute; something shocking in its brutal ugliness. What sort of perverse ritual was this, anyway? A confessional purging of primal moments or an excuse to dress as meat vendors? But there had been no crying or hugging, there had been the dispassionate recall of experience. Leonie had wrapped the intestine around her neck as she had told the story, revelling in its viscosity and decorating herself with its bulges like a necklace of unpopped seaweed. The others had been entertained when she had stood up and, with the ends sealed, had spun it around her head like a living lasso, whooping and catcalling at her stamping show. When the skin of the intestine had finally burst she scooped the muck up with her hands which she then wiped on the blue and white apron.

Crown thought she might throw up. There was the heart, the kidney and the brains to go. Crown pulled the heart towards her, moved most by the beautiful deep-red smoothness of it. All the women at the table sat watching her as she ran the pad of her index finger over the offal, not lifting or overturning it, not speaking. Crown's own heart was thumping in her ears, her throat swallowing to control the intermittent waves of nausea. What was required of her? She lifted her other hand into the enamel bowl and with a gentle action began to massage the heart with both hands. She did not squash or damage it, only closed her eyes to feel only the cold details of its shape.

'I remember when I was twenty-one in Germany and I had been hitchhiking around because it was considered safe there. I was coming from Cologne, trying to get to Trier, and it was getting very dark. I was starting to get desperate because I was out on this highway and I knew the once it got dark I would be stranded. But very few cars were on the road and none had stopped. Finally a semi-trailer stopped and I got in. Not being able to speak German, I smiled at the driver and enquired, "Trier?" and he nodded, unable to speak English. We drove for half an hour when I noticed him slowing down to pull over. I said, "Why are we stopping?" but he only smiled as the wheels crunched to a stop on the gravel and he turned off the vehicle. I sat rigid in my seat, as far from him as possible.

'He then lay his head down on the remaining expanse of the seat, his torso filling the space and his legs still underneath the wheel. I was at a loss to know what to do and was flagellating myself in my mind for not having paid for the train. Now what now what now what, panicked my brain. Ten minutes passed and he did nothing, while I sat, excruciated. The top of his hair brushed against my leg but it could have been nothing. When he put his legs up on the rest of the seat and tried to stretch out by pushing his head a little along the seat so that it was pressed against me I began to shake uncontrollably. A car pulled up in front of me and I leapt out of the cabin, dragging my pack with me as I ran towards it. I babbled to the driver, "Will you take me to the next town?" and he looked at me with shock. "Will you take me please please?" I tried not to seem too hysterical and vulnerable. He understood a little English and said, "Get in," and we drove away to the next town.'

Crown took her glass of water and poured it over her

hands into the enamel bowl. The heart swam in the mud-died liquid while she neatly wiped her hands on her apron. There was little or no stain. Janet got up out of her seat and began passing medals around the table. Crown could recognize the stripes and bows of war medallions being handed from one woman to another. Leonie passed her a medal and pinned one onto herself. There was still no discussion, but it seemed the party was coming to an end. Janet got up from the table and took the brain and kidney into another room. She removed Crown's heart on her way past and Meredith took the tripe and the liver in one hand each. Leonie was amusing herself by trying to use one of the war medals to repair the rupture of the intestine which still hung about her neck.

Crown got up and poured herself some more water from a half-full jug. She felt a sort of calm revulsion for the proceedings and wondered what the others had made of her story. Would she be invited again? She would come with her catalogue full of memory morsels. She smoothed the sleeves of her starched top and fiddled with the ties of her apron. Did they ever chop the offal on a wooden bench with a gleaming cleaver? Did they ever run it through with a skewer or a knife? Could you bring appliances to grind and mince and disguise its origin? Did they swap recipes on how to cook it in wines and creams and bitter sauce?

Janet was in an agony of irresponsibility. The fantastical notion of risk had seized her and her reality wobbled anarchically, like a spinning top that has lost its rhythm and veers drunkenly from side to side. As the women went into the bedroom to change out of their butchers' aprons, she saw that Meredith had her arm around Crown, gently rubbing her back. Janet picked up the brown, jellied brain and mentally ran through the story she wanted to find a way to tell.

'I remember I was walking down the street and this bloke came up to me and the woman I was with. He stopped us like, y'know, he was going to ask us the time or something. He stopped us and he says, "Excuse me," and I say, "Yeah," and he says, "Excuse me," and I just look at him and then he spits in my face. Whooo, like that. And he doesn't even run off and he just steps back and says, "Filthy dyke," and the women I'm with is about to grab him and he is walking backwards and he says, "I'll cut you bitches up next time," and then he goes to cross at the traffic lights and I'm wiping his shit from my face on my sleeve. He crosses the road and he screams out, "You're nothing."

'After it happened we backed into the entrance of a shop, where there was a mirror. We were looking at each other in the mirror, making faces and shrugging it off as though nothing bad had really happened. I particularly remember a sign in the shop with a huge, smiling, rotund man on it, a man with a sharpening pole in his hand. It calmed me down and I quickly thought, "It was nothing". My companion said, "Thanks for those thoughts, mate," and laughed. She hooked her arm in mine and we continued down the street.'

As she undid the ties of her butcher's apron, Janet knew that she would not bring this story to the table. Out of secrecy, Janet never spoke at her own offal parties. And the guests always somehow knew that she was exempted, just as they felt, for some inexplicable reason, a compulsion to contribute themselves.

CRYSTAL

NICK ENRIGHT

She smoulders. There is no other word for it. The continental cigarette in the corner of her overpainted mouth sends a thin column of smoke up into the rafters, but around her the air seems thick. From beneath a black beret, red hair of improbable lustre shadows one eye, falling onto a bottle-green sweater which clings to her breasts and shoulders as though applied with a spray-can. She turns to me, eyes glittering with disdain. I know you want me, she seems to say. And you know what the cost will be.

I don't want her. But the back of my neck prickles at the intimacy she has evoked with one weary exhalation, one shadowed glance. She may or may not be beautiful, but she has allure. I smile, to myself I hope, noting the campy overheated words she evokes. Smoulder. Lustre. Allure. Whatever the qualities, she is able to manifest them not in some smoky nightclub, or on some film noir street corner, but in the bright, even light of a Sydney autumn day.

We face one another across a dun-coloured lino floor. The room has windows on four sides, and on this bright day its rows of fluoros are dead. She ignores the others in the room. I can't shut them out, but they recede as I stare at her. She's amused by the silence, amused that the others sense it too. They are watching. I am watched. I stir in my plastic chair.

'And who are you?' I ask, cool, magisterial.

She pauses before answering. 'Crystal.'

'What do you want to tell us about yourself, Crystal?'

'Not much.' Eyes glitter like aquamarines. She drags on a Sobranie, coughs lightly. A couple of others giggle. She stares them down and starts to talk. She has tried to make a go of it as a model and party girl, she has lived hard. Now she's in recovery. She has decided to become an actress.

Several watchers stifle a giggle. The basilisk eyes make a swift circuit of the room. I ask what sort of roles she's after. For the first time she smiles. She slicks her lips with the point of her tongue.

'What sort of role did you have in mind, sweetie?'

She crushes her cigarette on the floor with the toe of a sleek red shoe. She goes back to her corner. Her place in the centre is taken by a man in a suit. I take command. 'Who are you?'

Ralph is an office worker who has experienced long bouts of unemployment. Underqualified in today's tough market, he suffers from low self-esteem. Crystal sighs, raising pencilled eyebrows at me. Low self-esteem is not Crystal's problem. She wills me to keep looking at her. I train my eyes back on Ralph, noting his thin moustache, incongruous against pale beardless skin, his throaty voice trembling with the effort of assertion.

Ralph is followed by Maria, a socialite with a viscous Hungarian accent; Jelko, an apprentice mechanic in overalls; Vicky, a gangly receptionist from a real estate office. Maria and Jelko and Vicky claim their time, tell their stories, but they sense that the strongest presence in the room is still Crystal's. She seems to propel each of them to the centre of the room, patting Jelko's arm, adjusting Vicky's Sportsgirl outfit, murmuring honeyed words of reassurance. Then, as each takes the floor and starts to speak, she stares, eyes dead, gashy mouth askew, murmuring some secret obscenity that the whole room longs to hear.

Once, Maria, braver than Ralph and Jelko and Vicky, tries to stare her down. Crystal thrives on a diet of challenge. She meets the other woman's glare. The red gash widens. 'What's your problem, bitch-features?'

Maria appeals to me. Is this fair? Is this right? I shrug. What can I do? Crystal rules. I try to be fair, as I always try to be, as I am paid to be, giving credence to the others and their desire to reveal themselves. But they must feel my interest veering towards the woman in the beret and sweater and the tight black skirt.

Of course Crystal is not a biological woman. But then, neither is socialite Maria, whose solid soccer-player's legs show beneath the borrowed silk jersey dress. Nor is Vicky, the tall receptionist swaying on her (daring, borrowed) platforms. Jelko, the mechanic, is not a man, not even Croatian. Ralph, the office worker in the pale polyester suit, peels off a pencil moustache at the end of the session. Underneath his sweat-stained jacket is the outline of a real, ample female bosom.

And these five are not the only pretenders. Sitting around the walls, hanging off the dance-bar, leaning in the windows, are a dozen other faux-men, faux-women. Housewife, bus-driver, croupier, waitress, their names and occupations are borrowed like their clothes, their sex. Alone in the room, I am what I seem to be: a 32-year-old man answering to my own name, dressed as a man, in my own clothes, doing what I truly do, teaching the art of acting.

I say the art of acting. I am no amateur therapist. My students are not weekend wannabes, but part of a famous school. I am a respected teacher, cited as a formative influence by graduates in press interviews. And on this Friday morning in autumn I am conducting the second of three classes on the empathetic portrayal of the opposite sex. That's too big a phrase for the timetable. There it says: 11.30, Character (Drag). Those brackets hold other topics at other times. Enter this room earlier in the year and you will see Old Age; later, it may be High Status. Last week, this week and next week, it's Drag. My favourite.

For my students the assignment is both ordeal and delight. The classes have the same pattern each year. At the first the women make their fictive men rough-spoken yobbos, while the men turn girlish. Afterwards, each sex nails the other: is that how you see us? Discussion leads to laughter, argument, revelation. We talk of yin and yang, of our male and female sides. The second session always shows results. Parody has yielded to empathy.

And so it is this year. Ralph is an ordinary bloke with commonplace concerns, his manhood muted by a sad shyness. Jelko has woman trouble. We laugh, but we believe him. Vicky worries about her height, has difficulty finding boyfriends. We are sympathetic. Even fulsome Maria, with her perilously comic accent, has vulnerability. Only Crystal bends the rules. Her truculence, her moues and flounces, have redefined the class, shaken its foundation in empathy. This is somewhat unnerving.

It's one o'clock. Some shed bits of their disguise. All begin to head down the stairs. I close the windows and pick up styrofoam cups, forgotten furbelows. This high, drab space overlooks a racecourse, and the jumble of rooms on the two floors below us are said to be the old changing-rooms for jockeys and strappers. Now, as a westerly brings the faint, dank smell of manure off the exercise yard, the old rooms will be full of boys discarding bras stuffed with toilet paper, sliding out of sweaty pantyhose; girls washing out hair gel, applying cleanser to painted sideburns. I stare across the racecourse.

The stairs are narrow and steep, and the room takes some time to empty. Tom, who was Crystal only minutes ago, is last to leave. Is he hanging back? Without Crystal's anima, his painted lips and eyelids look ridiculous. He has no tissues to wipe them. He licks nervously, as though aware of what the scarlet gash does to his face.

He is hanging back. He has unhooked the bra beneath the sweater, and his false breasts are askew. They might be a cancerous growth under the green wool. He looks bizarre, neither Crystal nor Tom.

He sees me staring at him, or past him to the vanished creature. He's been my student for fifteen months and I don't believe I have ever stared at him before. He's a sweet-natured country boy with a light tenor voice and a wiry body. He goes out with but does not live with a female design student. At its best his work has great freshness, at its worst a stodgy sincerity. Nothing has prepared his classmates for today's creation. Last week he presented a sweet-natured country girl, a boarder at Abbotsleigh, doubt-less modelled on his own sister. The short tunic and pale blue eyes stirred some mild erotic interest in the rest of the room, but I found his creation as dull as ditchwater. I said so. I urged him to take a leap, to get out on the edge. I spoke of yin and yang. This was Tom's opportunity to challenge his sense of himself, if he was ready for a challenge. Mindful that assessment time is near, he declared himself ready. And this week, today, in walked Crystal.

Now Tom is walking out, barefoot, clutching the wig, the coat, the large red shoes. For the first time I look through the pantyhose to see the smooth shaved legs. 'What did you think of Crystal?' Like all the group he has learned from me to place his characters in the clinical third person. 'Was she on the edge?'

'She's tragic.' I smile. He smiles, gratified. He drops one shoe, gathers it up and hurries down the stairs to lunch. I close the last window, breathing in the rich smell from the racecourse. In the stable yard across the street two apprentice jockeys unload feedsacks from the back of a truck. I linger in the room a few minutes longer, till I remember a staff meeting.

Tom stands under the Moreton Bay figs in the yard, with an arm round Jelko. Tall Vicky, now restored to reality as Brad, a gymnast with an awesome physique, passes Tom, pinching his arse. All three laugh. I hurry to my meeting.

But its administrative issues scarcely touch me. I answer questions mechanically. I am still in the upper room with those hooded aquamarine eyes. Even the afternoon class doesn't engage me, and I teach perfunctorily for four hours. Then I head home in the autumn twilight.

I spend Saturday with *Hedda Gabler*. I've looked forward to this prospect for years, but now I stare at the stark, white floor and blood-red walls on the cardboard model, wondering why these decisions seemed so sensible, so sensitive a week ago. I lose faith. For the first time it strikes me that my designer, Jane, is the girl who goes out with but probably does not live with Tom. Now I wonder if she dressed Crystal, coiffed and styled and made her up. Such a transformation must have called on an outside eye, a designer's eye. Wouldn't it?

I make strong coffee, slice a honeydew melon into slim segments, open my script, try to fix myself on nineteenth-century Norway, though Jane's setting has placed us nowhere, in no time. I wonder why everything is red and white, why the setting seems to be a kind of tunnel. Jane talked about the uterus, the heroine's fear of childbirth.

'Yes, yes,' I said, 'brilliant. Let's go with it.' Now I've gone with it. Sweet-natured recessive Tom will be Judge Brack, a good stretch for him, the staff said. I wonder how Crystal would go as Hedda Gabler. I see that slow, sullen smile, those drowsy eyes, that swan neck, the overpainted mouth drawing on the black cigarette. (Tom is not a smoker.) I find I've been chewing along the pale-green rind of a melon slice. I throw it in the bin, drain the dregs of my coffee and begin to work. I have remarkable powers of discipline. All my students say so.

On Monday afternoon, we start work on the play. Tom is as he was, sweet, affable, slight. As we read, it's clear that my Judge Brack is out of his depth. I comfort myself that the Hedda is excellent, supple and imaginative. We will collaborate well. Jane presents the costume designs. The students are surprised. They were expecting bustles and high collars. But though the setting is no-time no-place, the clothes relocate Ibsen's stuffy community in a provincial Australian university town—Armidale, say, in the early 1950s. Jane has a good eye, and renders her figures well. Hedda looks stylish: the New Look comes to New England. I watch Tom's response to the sketches. He studies the Brack design, which he must surely have seen if he lives with Jane (does he live with Jane?) but seems uninterested in the women's clothes.

We make a good beginning. Jane is in the room on Tuesday afternoon when we analyse Judge Brack's idea of a 'triangular arrangement'. Hedda's husband (gymnastic Brad) wonders if the Judge means that he, Tesman, will be 'the meat in the sandwich'. My Hedda laughs throatily, peeling a mandarin. Jane is also amused. Other views are offered. Tom stays silent. We read the scene again. None of the discussion seems to have touched him. When he reaches the phrase he lets it pass without any carnal nuance.

On Wednesday we take the floor. By the time Tom is on his feet I have forgotten last Friday's apparition. I see an attractive dullish boy with good prospects in television, struggling to comprehend a great role and through it the mysterious art of transformation.

Thursday brings Friday morning near, too near. I feel mild anxiety, but also a sense of fluttery apprehension. On Thursday night I flout my weekday regimen and open a bottle of red wine. My head is fuzzy when I drive in on Friday. But I remind myself sternly, I know how to teach.

I do know how to teach. And I know how to orchestrate these sessions. By the third week, the room will be alive with laughter and relaxed observation, half laboratory and half music-hall. The participants will feel a sense of achievement. They will have essayed different modes of vocal and physical expression. They will have inspected the fences along their psychic boundaries. Near the end, (quarter to one) we will deconstruct the experience. Yin and yang will get another run. We will speak of the construction of femaleness and maleness, of assigned social roles, and, more cautiously, of sexual ambivalence and its place in our work. I will cite the great androgynes, Cagney and Dietrich and Hepburn. I will invoke Shakespeare, and Noh theatre. I will offer to lend videos of *Some Like It Hot*, *Sylvia Scarlett*, *Viktor und Viktoria*. At lunchtime, wigs and moustaches will be shed, shoes slipped off for the last time. They will go down the stairs. The game will be over for another year.

But this year in the high, drab room it ends badly. I get through the remaining interviews efficiently enough. And they're good, the best yet. Russell is a skinhead who wants to be a master chef. Penny is a physiotherapist. Stavros (my Hedda, Greek herself, audacious and supple as ever) is a nightclub manager with a thatch of chest hair.

Last comes a woman in slacks and halter top. No

makeup. A stroller with a sleeping child. Margie is a barmaid whose husband is a transvestite. Margie (a quiet student, the best transformer among the men) manages to make this painful revelation simply, without throwing us into a dizzy self-referential spiral. An ordinary woman describes a life with a husband who is savage and uncommunicative except when in travesty. It's a risky, delicate creation. The room falls silent. Then Crystal mutters something out of the side of that maddening, painted mouth. The people nearby giggle. I ask Crystal to repeat the comment. Crystal shakes her head. I push the moment.

'Crystal, tell Margie what you said.' Down in the exercise yard, two jockey boys are tussling. One turns the hose on the other.

Crystal lights her cigarette (this week a mere Marlboro) and stares back coolly. She takes the challenge, steps out from the window. Margie looks wanly at her.

'How tall is he, sweetie?' Margie, a tall boy, hesitates, then indicates someone of her own height. 'So what's your problem? You've doubled your wardrobe.' Crystal flashes a citric smile, flicks ash in the direction of the stroller and turns on her heel. A single tear courses down Margie's cheek. She doesn't want to say any more.

Loathing Crystal, applauding both for maintaining their shared reality, I decide to change the mood, test them all. We take a walk. Authoritatively, quickly, I chart the new game. Where could they all conceivably meet? The foyer at Hoyts.

'You're early for the movie. Find a reason to make contact with one stranger.' Some sit, some stride, some pace. Stavros edges closer to Vicky. Ralph asks Russell for advice about what movie to see. Ralph recommends Jim Carrey's latest. Crystal stares at Margie, who moves away, nearly bumping into Maria, who is mistaking a squat banker for a man she met at the ballet. It's working well. I slide into a corner between two windows. Jelko asks Crystal for a light. She stares through him. He moves on. They're all making contact, everyone but Crystal. It's twelve-thirty. Soon it will all be over.

At twelve-forty, I prepare to terminate this display of invention. Ralph has trouble with his folding umbrella. Penny loses her ticket and turns her purse upside down on the floor, to Margie's distress. Stavros seems to have persuaded Vicky to accompany him to the new Bruce Willis.

Suddenly, Crystal is in front of me. Close. Too close. This is against the rules. I'm not with them all at Hoyts. I'm somewhere else, an invisible observer. She exhales in my face. I quit, famously and successfully, two years ago, so the gust of smoke is doubly offensive. I stare her down. Her eyes narrow. Nobody else can hear her. (Jelko is talking to Margie. The mess round Penny gets bigger.) Crystal leans closer. I scowl, more or less in the moment. 'Go away.'

She doesn't move. She holds my gaze. 'You like to lose control. Don't you, sweetie?' Rage surges through me. I freeze. A single fingernail traverses my chest, tracing a line from thorax to belt-buckle. Rage is turning to something else. Her finger stops at my buckle, hovers a moment, withdraws. She pushes back a strand of auburn hair. I can see only one hooded eye. 'Come and see me.' And she's gone.

I look at my watch. It's late, ten to one. I muff the final debriefing. I get lost in the social construction of sexuality. The students are polite but confused. My mouth is dry. I feel her fingernail stroking down my sternum and my belly, which I held hard (vanity or tension?) as the touch descended. Lunchtime comes. The students seem to shed their borrowed gear gratefully, as though the exercise has been an ordeal without pleasure. And this time, this last time, as they file down the stairs Crystal does not look back.

At lunchtime I go for a run, slipping through the exercise yard, past the apprentices and the sleek, silly horses, over a fence to an outlying section of the empty track. I always drive myself hard, proud that my reprieved lungs will take the strain. Today I drive harder, so hard and long that I am late for the afternoon rehearsal.

The student stage manager patiently applies a template to pages of script, tracing the contours of walls and furniture. Tom and Hedda sit alone in the middle of the floor. He kneads her shoulders while she loosens her jaw and neck. A stranger might mistake them for lovers, but hours of shared physical and emotional exertion give actors an easy, sexless intimacy. The stage manager glances at them hungrily, feeling the ache of exclusion. The pair rise easily to their feet. I mumble an apology. I tell the truth. They smile politely. They know about my running. As I pass through the courtyard I occasionally make jokes about my legs, which are long and limber for a man of middle height. Brad has been known to whistle.

Today we abandon the text to do an exercise I call Boundary Riding. The medium can be mime, or dance, or gibberish or animal behaviour; the aim is to explore the components of character. I don't direct, I facilitate. The students choose the territory. Hedda wants to explore status. Daughter of two suburban restaurateurs, she wants to feel what it is to be General Gabler's daughter.

I turn to Tom. Our eyes meet for the first time since the fingernail traversed my upper body. He is, as always, deferential, affable, the provincial GP's son. Crystal has vanished forever. I centre myself. I am calm. I ask Tom which boundary he wants to ride.

'Well, I don't know. He's got high status in the town.

He's good with words. I suppose he's an intellectual. And he's a bit of a perv.' The stage manager looks up from the prompt copy. She giggles. Tom makes a face at her. Hedda laughs that throaty laugh which will be her signature in years to come. I smile. I facilitate our way from perv to sexual predator. The work begins.

An hour later, two things are clear. Hedda, a natural actress, clearly apprehends status with the instinct of a diva, and takes on the air of a Callas or a Stratas. But Tom is no perv, no predator, whether Brack transforms into tomcat or flasher or giant licking tongue.

He starts to punish himself in the way of student actors, pounding the dance-bar, kicking the skirting-board. I take him aside. I am quiet encouraging. I have a suggestion which may ease the way. 'We need to see Crystal in the room.'

He looks blank for a long moment, as though asked to recall some distant stranger. Then he strokes his hairless chin. His unpainted mouth seems oddly small. 'How do you mean?'

How do I mean? 'You tapped into something with her. Something you can use here.' He looks puzzled. Over his shoulder, Hedda radiates empathy for me. If she were older she would roll her eyes. But the boy is ingenuous. He truly doesn't see it. I cut to the chase.

'Do the scene as Crystal.'

'As Crystal?'

The stage manager sits up. She hasn't met Crystal, but something in the hard bright sound alerts her for what may follow.

Nothing does follow. He lowers his eyes. What am I seeing? Is it shame? Or a kind of protective pride? 'You need the gear for that.'

'Then get the gear.'

'I've given it all back.' To whom? I bite my lip on the question. He's staring at me. It strikes me that Tom thinks I'm the predator. The perv. Unfair. He put the move on me. That is not quite true. *He* didn't. I take command. We will break for coffee, then rehearse the scene. The text may release something for him.

After coffee, the work doesn't improve. But our maxim here is that everything is process. He avoids my eye for the rest of the day. I feel choked. Nobody would know it, though the stage manager seems suddenly watchful, and once I think I intercept a glance between the two on the floor.

I drive home in a light rain. On Triple J the Smiths sing 'Please Please Please Let Me Get What I Want'. I switch to Drivetime. The rain thickens.

I go out drinking with my friend Danny, but walk home alone in the rain. It's nearly midnight. I need a shower, a joint, another drink, I don't know what. I take up the spring-binder that holds my script. I see a column of addresses and numbers.

The gutters in the little street are overflowing, the drains clogged with plane tree leaves. I find the number with a torch, park outside the house, a frowsty single-storey terrace. There's a light in the hall. I take the keys out of the ignition. He'll be out at the pub. If he's in, she'll be there. He'll be sharing with others. They'll be partying at the back of the house. At the top of my bag is my script in its spring-binder. I pick up the bag.

He answers the door. The house feels frigid. He wears a hand-knitted sweater, tracksuit pants, football socks, a beanie. The light is behind him. I can't tell if he's pleased or embarrassed. His body registers surprise. I say I wanted to see if he was all right after this afternoon. Puzzled but polite, he leads me down the hall.

He turns down the music and the house is silent. A

single-bar radiator burns in front of a boarded-up fireplace. On the cracked plaster walls are hand-stencilled bills for a band called Dead Poke Society. There's a Metallica poster, a bright yellow DMR barrier complete with lanterns, and, incongruous in the corner, an Ansel Adams landscape. A can of VB sits on an old trunk I recognise from my *Cherry Orchard*, a lovingly detailed production, greatly successful. The only other furniture is an orange vinyl lounge suite, ripped and scuffed. After a moment, I recognise this from someone else's production of *The Removalists*. We are silent. Tom offers coffee. Seeing the tin of International Roast on the sink I decline.

I wonder how much time I have before his housemates return. Circuitous enquiry reveals that he shares with Brad, who's gone to spend the weekend with his girlfriend in Wollongong. We have time to ourselves. I put the script and bag down. He glances at it, fearing what lies ahead. I reassure him. This is not work. We are not at school, not bound by its rules. I simply want to talk to him. What about?

About Crystal, I say. The name makes him nervous. My voice is calm reassurance. It's important for us both to see Crystal again, to bring her back. She has much to teach us. He's not following me. I say I want to see her. She disappeared. I have to see Crystal. I hear my voice, louder than I mean it to be, discomfiting this nice-mannered boy. We're standing close. With a rush, I see his mistake. He fears some kind of lateral move is being made on him. I put my hands on his knobbly shoulders to reassure him. He actually recoils. I'm not handling this well. I sit. He asks if I'm okay. If I'm okay. I pull a bundle out from my bag.

Five years ago, Danny tried to dress me up for a dance party, make me over as a flash-trash Cindy Lauper clone. We argued, I held firm, and he stormed off, leaving the outfit. Here it is now, spread out on the old trunk, wig and skirt and top and shoes, pantyhose still musty, as though long unwashed. A new look for Crystal, I say. A makeover.

He stares at me. Deference wrestles with indignation. 'For rehearsals?' Now, I say, now. Try it. He shakes his head. Put these on, I say, you'll learn so much about yourself. The triangular arrangement, you had no idea. You'll understand it. Please, please. The can of VB which I thought was empty is knocked over, spills on the carpet. I mop it up with my handkerchief. Please, I say. Crystal can't just say that to me and go, disappear, walk out.

'Say what?' He can't have forgotten. He's playing with me. He sits on the couch, aping concern. He puts a hand, one chaste polite hand, on my shoulder. I thrust the gear at him. The hair's a different colour, I say, but Crystal can take it. She's that kind of girl. Do it. Just do it. He won't take the bundle. He's angry, almost tearful. He pushes me away. He tells me to go. Please go. Get out. I can't. Do it. Do it. Do it. Who is making that noise? There are footsteps in the hall. He said he was alone. He lied to me. Jane stands in the door with a Domino pizza box. She stares. He's on the floor with me. His nose is bleeding. He drops blood onto Crystal's hair.

The head of the school, an understanding woman who admired my *Cherry Orchard*, suggests that no public announcement be made. The production is taken over by a colleague who is thought to be good at damage control. I spend the winter at Danny's Aunt Lulla's house in the mountains. Several letters of puzzled condolence reach me, one of them from my Hedda, who sends a polaroid of herself as Stavros, chest hair and all. I don't write back, but silently wish her the career she deserves.

Now I am here in Armidale, a tutor in an academic course. They tell me they are lucky to have me. I enliven my seminars with practical work, and after some weeks the students, even the shyest, are eager to participate. On the floor the material comes alive for them. I try new exercises. They respond well. They like me, I think. I never drop names of famous former students. I am here for them and them alone, facilitating, not directing. My classes are crowded. My head of department takes me aside. The students are clamouring for me to take the work a step further. I smile, shake my head. Before he can argue, I stride off home. In the Northern Tablelands autumn comes quickly, and I wind my scarf round my neck, kicking through the leaves in the pale sunshine.

Tsunami

FIONA MCGREGOR

Sydney, 1985

That summer was his first in the city. Through the corridor of shops and houses lining the hill he could see the ocean, flat, heavy, a strip of metallic white across the horizon where the sun hit the water way off-shore. The clouds were so low they seemed to graze the roof of the bus as it hurtled down the last steep section of Bondi Road and turned into the wide marine curve, buildings dropping away. He pressed his torso against the rail and steadied his surfboard in the luggage rack. Everybody squinted and the bus grew silent as the beach stretched below. There was no breeze when he walked down the grass slope through squalling seagulls.

It wasn't always going to be like this. Later the swells would rise to meet the promises his sister had made, but this was how he would always think of Bondi. Still, leaden ocean, windless; Mediterranean waves. So many shapes, sizes and colours of people that he couldn't believe they all lived here. He sat there till midday, smoking away his appetite, watching bars of new colour roll slowly in beneath the water as the cloud bank lifted and pulled back over the city.

He was at the Exchange Hotel, legless from the last snort of amyl and too many Pernod and cokes. Tiles cold against his cheek, his vision gradually returned showing him a pair of Doc Martens being relaced on the other side of the door.

Out by the bar, the red-haired electrician waits. He's rapt. In just an hour he's lost his senses, gone crazy for this scorched 16-year-old skin, the sea-stiffened hair, teeth bleached patchily by childhood penicillin.

The boy stayed on the floor, no money left, dreaming of a daiquiri. He'd give another smile for that. The red-haired electrician brought him down here from the park. That was a mistake. Don't talk to them, let alone have a drink, don't bother, not even your name; just do up your fly then walk away across the grass.

He was there another night. It had become regular—the beach, the park, this bar. He went home only to get clean clothes and work his two days at the newsagency, knowing he was beyond reproach. It was school holidays and his mother had a new boyfriend, Warren. Warren the Rat, he called him, because of the way he sniffed around the house, eyes darting here and there as though he was sizing up the furniture, as though he thought he'd soon be selling it in his crummy second-hand furniture shop. Fat chance, Ratso.

He came out of the toilet first. She was bent over near the basin fixing the final knot on her shin-high Docs, Annie Lennox hair poking into his leg. She was wearing puffy shorts in rich satin and velvet that reminded him of Henry the Eighth. She straightened up and looked him in the eye, grinning. 'Was it good?' she said, then turned to her reflection and re-blackened her lips. He was offended until he saw the glance of hatred shot at her by the guy who'd just blown him, on his way back out to the bar. There were hardly any girls here, let alone in the toilets, let alone who looked like her. He stopped and stood beside her, washing his hands, curious. Just before she went out he said to her, with all the aplomb of a man who'd been around, 'I've had better.'

Another night he was there, and she was there too, black-haired instead of blonde. Seemed they always ran into each other in the men's toilets at the Exchange. They smirked at the mirror, sharing the tap water, then he left, letting the thick wooden door swing back behind him. She caught it and pushed. 'Hey Holmes, wanna drink?' Handing him his school bus pass, retrieved from the muddy floor. He patted his back pocket in surprise. Holmes. The only other person who'd ever called him that was Mr Radziowski, his maths teacher. His ex-maths teacher. *School's out forever!* She made his surname sound different, more adult, exotic. It was like being christened. This was his new life.

Billy said she used the men's toilets because the women's were always full of drag queens queuing at the mirror and she hated waiting. If she had to make a hate list, that'd be in the top five—waiting. And lavender. Lavender? Holmes thought of the old Crystal Cylinders sweatshirt he still wore, cut-off sleeves, faded to lavender. He put his chin in his hand and noticed his fingers still smelt of coconut hair wax. Over by the mirror the man wearing the wax was still trying to look alluring. Holmes watched Billy.

She was eighteen, she was legal. He thought she was older but once she'd said her age, it suited her. She'd left home three years ago, making Holmes feel like a late starter. Billy cleaned for a living but making outfits was what she lived for. The shorts were nothing: she'd recently made a pair of one-foot-high platforms from cardboard and fibreglass then danced all night in them. She had a cigarette voice and eyebrows plucked to one thin line. Sometimes she shaved them right off, she said, sometimes she even waxed them. Holmes' teeth ground against ice and his tongue went numb. He couldn't tell what Billy's real colouring was. Her eyes, round, sad and surprised beneath those fine-line eyebrows neatened with a pencil; lashes dipped in mascara, shock of black hair, or, as he'd once seen it already, white. Her skin was, well . . . bluish, considering he'd only ever seen her at night, in this bar.

She called him Holmes, or any of its derivatives, Homie, Home Boy, Homer Hudson ice-cream. Or just Ice-Cream. Most of the names sounded like terms of endearment, most of them he liked. Sixty-Nine was another name she used, after the year of his birth and a story he told her one of those first nights at the Exchange, when she touched the scratch on the back of his neck questioningly. About going to Centennial Park on the way home from the beach, getting done behind a Moreton Bay fig. How the guy dragged Holmes down to suck him as well so they ended up having a sixty-niner and Holmes, on the bottom, when his head tipped back in orgasm, gouged his neck on a stick jammed beneath his shoulder. Holmes sensed that by naming him, Billy was in some way claiming him. He didn't mind this, belonging to her, but Sixty-Nine wasn't really him. It referred to the least real part of him, to his after-hours self, not his full-time self.

He was a 16-year-old surfie boy from the northern beaches, crossing the bridge for the first time this summer because he hated the gangs that ruled the waves he grew up on. He hated their girlfriends locked into submission, checking their bikini lines, checking up on him, forcing stories afterwards from the girls he took behind the dunes—the least pretty, the quietest—pinning them flat on the burning sand, knees into elbows and another holding the legs. Did he finger you? Did you do it? I knew it. Frigid. Have ya seen the way he looks at Matt? Somehow Holmes expected more of the girls. Male threat had always been there. He understood the combativeness of boys and, later, men. The hunting gaze that could mean a blow or an embrace, and you wouldn't know until you were in their mouth; desire was fear. Crossing the bridge, too, because on the south side there was the activity he'd discovered by chance at a Dire Straits concert. A man followed him from the dark hall then they were alone in the vast toilets, the man feeling himself. Holmes knew to leave the door open. It only took ten minutes and not a word was spoken—pleasure was never easier. There were beats on the North Shore too but it didn't occur to Holmes to seek them out.

Sometimes, sitting at the bar (Holmes keeping out of the light in case they asked him for ID), he and Billy played Spot The Dyke. Once they saw another dyke there. A real diesel. Another time there were two girls who they thought were dykes—two post-punkettes in tartan minis and leather jackets. But then their boyfriends came in. Billy groaned.

School holidays, Monday blurring to Sunday. Holmes stayed at his sister's place in Paddington. She put his board in her room and him on the couch. He crept upstairs and climbed into her bed the nights she stayed at her boyfriend's. It was hard sleeping there at first, the Glenmore Road traffic, headlights through french windows scanning the wax-pocked surface of his Malibu. The scuttling of cockroaches in the dark kitchen when he went down for 3 a.m. orange juice made his skin crawl. He opened the windows when he slept there, but the living room never lost its bitter smell of marijuana ashtrays.

Outside Lizzie's bedroom window was a big desert oak. The wind rushing through it sounded like distant surf, a tide constantly rising, and Holmes went to sleep dreaming of waves, seven footers, glittering in the sun, him in the tube, ride after ride. One night Lizzie had a fight with her boyfriend. She came home and threw Holmes out of her bed. A sudden spill of light behind her dark head, framed by red-gold curls as she stood over him, furious. I didn't say you could sleep in my *bed*, Peter. What made him angry—it wasn't being moved back down to the couch—was her voice. As though he heard it for the first time, pronouncing his pedestrian first name. How perfect it sounded, how nice. And as he descended through the dark house his sister altered in his eyes. The adult world was not one formidable mass, inaccessible, on the other side of a divide. It was an ants' nest crumbling towards him and he was falling down a tunnel towards Billy, her mess and her danger. He was heading for the arcane recesses of homo lust, away from Lizzie and her perfect intonation, her lecture notes and dinner parties.

Holmes and Billy took plates or plastic containers down to the Hare Krishnas after five. They ate quickly, looking out at Billy's view over William Street to western Sydney and the sky's final fire. Holmes had read nothing, he had heard nothing, about the gay scene in this city or any other. He had no expectations and so absorbed everything without question, events occurring just as they should occur. This was how it was then: one lone dyke at its centre, conspicuous as a rainbow, and him, a teenage boy, in a sea of men. There were bars and beats, back streets and Billy's studio, never much money or routine of any sort, drugs the only luxury. Within weeks he loved disco and had sold his rock and ska records. They cruised around Oxford Street, Billy pointing out the clubs and bars. Up ahead, a group of guys in leather who Billy waved to, the stairs behind them leading up to a fuck club. Further down Crown there was another, heavy duty, where Billy couldn't go either. Holmes said he wouldn't dream of it. There was a dyke bar but it wasn't open every night and they didn't let men in. Besides, Billy said it was a real dive. Butch was fine but they hated leather. As for women's dances, the last time Billy went to one, wearing a headdress of a birdcage containing her pet rainbow lorikeet, she got spat on by an animal liberationist. The bird died a year later of old age. They drank at the Oxford sometimes, but the men could be hostile to Billy. So back down to the Exchange they would go, back to the corner of the bar from where they could see everyone. Holmes with his chin in his hands talking to Billy, imagining smooth divots slowly forming in the wooden counter beneath his elbows.

She asked him about his trade, she wanted to know all the details: size, weight, age, hairiness, the places and the times and what exactly they did, who instigated it. These were the salacious conversations he would later associate with men huddled around beers, sniggering and groaning. Billy shook her head and smiled. 'You guys've really got it made, you know, Homo.'

'Don't call me that.'

'Sor-ry.'

Billy lived in a hot, light studio opposite the fire station at the top of the hill. Pink feathers littered the stairs to her door on the third storey. It was often ajar, Billy standing by the window, foot on the pedal of her sewing machine. Holmes visited almost daily, sometimes he stayed with her, sleeping back to back, waking one dawn with her belly beneath his hand. His fingertips explored the length of his torso, the pulse in her neck and her warm slow breath. She was sleek like a seal, the first female body he'd touched so completely, a layer of firm flesh beneath the soft skin, unlike his which could be pinched and lifted from any part of his body. When she woke he snatched his hand back. Billy pulled on jeans and a T-shirt and went to clean.

She cleaned an apartment in Elizabeth Bay, three in

Potts Point, and a mansion belonging to two leather queens in Paddington. Even their feather dusters were luxurious, dove-white plumes, soft against her cheeks. She used them on the cabinet containing a collection of dildos and butt plugs. There were Dutch ones, English ones, French, American; there was an antique lacquered one from Imperial Japan with decorations so intricate they could have been painted with a needle. Holmes listened to her descriptions in awe—everything Billy did seemed like an adventure; he even wanted to come to her cleaning jobs. But mornings vanished hidden beneath the bedclothes, chasing imaginary waves.

Billy went through her clothes to find Holmes something to wear. Holmes unpeeled a banana and perched on the desk, watching her. He'd been wearing the same jeans for weeks now, two pairs he alternated. And three big T-shirts. Billy waded into the alcove, knee deep in garments. She stood and held against herself a ballgown made of latex, fine and translucent. When she waltzed towards him, then waltzed back to the alcove, Holmes glimpsed paraphernalia stitched among the folds: condoms, syringes, lipstick, lighter, small notebook, some dollar notes. He dressed her in his mind and floated her through tall, painted rooms, watching from her eyes the powdered wigs turn and stare, till Billy rose again suddenly from her pile, terrifying him in a mask made from a horse's jawbones placed either side of the face, wired together at the protruding ends, wax mould set deep between them over her eyes, nose and mouth. Holmes squealed and bit his fingers. Then Billy showed him a garment called the Timezone Suit: a red body stocking decorated with plastic clocks over each breast, large lifelike ticks embedded in the armpits and what looked like an egg-timer over the crotch. 'What's that?' Holmes pointed to it.

'The time of your life,' Billy grinned, then threw it to the back of the alcove and kept on searching. She pulled out a piece of orange tuile, a hard hat, green lurex trousers. No no no. Vinyl mini. I doubt it. Leather jeans. She threw them over to Holmes. Holmes hopped off the desk and stripped down to his Y-fronts, the banana skin dropping onto the floor. 'You've lost weight, Sixty-Nine,' said Billy, watching him sorrowfully as he puffed out his chest.

Holmes flexed his pecs and winced. He'd felt the strain yesterday at Bondi, paddling out for the first time in a week. The surf was big—king tides, freak swells—and it took him ages to get out the back. He'd duck-dived and lost the board to the wave, and saw now that his ankle was still raw where it had been strangled by the leg rope. He'd caught one wave—a big mother, eight foot—and felt the heaviness of fear move swiftly along his limbs. He got out of the water immediately and sat smoking on the beach, feet burrowed into the hot sand. Holmes lost weight with the alacrity of an anxious teenage boy, and looking down his body was shocked by the salient pelvis and narrow thighs. He picked up the jeans. Their smell, their weight, skin on skin. He pulled them on and did up the button fly. Tight on Billy, waist high, they sat loosely on Holmes hips. He turned this way and that, light frilling the downy aureoles around his small nipples, ridging along his stomach muscles. The leather jeans made him feel like sex, like he was it, not just wanted it. Billy whistled, she turned up Prince and cheered as Holmes swayed and strutted. He stopped in front of the full length mirror. 'Do I look like you?'

'Hmm,' Billy squinted. 'You'd have to tuck.'

'If I was a girl I'd want to look like you.'

'If I was a boy I'd want to look like you.'

'Oh no, Billy,' Holmes shook his head. 'You wouldn't want to be a boy.'

'Dykes are so boring, sometimes I wish I was a poof.'

'Poofs are so up themselves sometimes, I wish I was a dyke.'

Billy pointed to the banana skin as he shimmied across the floor towards her. 'Make sure you don't slip.'

Friday night was drag night at Patches. They walked down the street holding hands, watching the gays hesitate and enjoying their confusion, because Billy and Holmes couldn't look more queer and yet they seemed like lovers.

At Patches Holmes felt like he was in *La Cage aux Folles*, they all looked so old, and Gloria Gaynor always blazing through the speakers with 'I Am What I Am'. Billy got the drinks while Holmes watched two men dancing hip to hip across the chequered dancefloor, the fluid line of their bodies, how beautiful they looked.

At their table a Maori transsexual cheered and whistled as the lights went down. The star of the show was regally tall, taller than her dancing boys. As she wheeled around the stage lip-syncing to Donna Summer, her skirt rose and she pushed it coyly back down between her thighs. Holmes was sweating, lips sucked in tight around his teeth. Billy came back from the bar empty-handed, saying there were free drinks for all those in drag. The tranny plucked the yellow umbrella from her drink and twirled it with her thumb and forefinger, looking from Holmes to Billy and back again, eyebrows raised. Her voice was dark and slow, like molasses. 'Isn't it past your bedtime, sweet thing?' she said to Holmes, then to Billy, 'Bit risky bringing your boyfriend here, isn't it girlie? Or are you a boy?'

Holmes followed Billy into the girls' toilet. Billy knew the drag in there, a Thursday Islander called Jackson who wore black leggings and a tight Pepsi T-shirt. Jackson told Billy there were girls here tonight, not just tranny girls, girl girls too, and Billy whistled. Jackson agreed to lend them her tits—plastic inflatables that stuck to the skin—until the free drinks were over. Billy took off her skirt, leaving black stockings and the knee-high Docs. She swapped her black T-shirt with Holmes' leopard print long-sleeved shirt which came down to the tops of her thighs. She wet her hair and slicked it back, wiped off her lipstick and pencilled a Clark Gable moustache across her upper lip, then she thickened her eyebrows. 'Here.' Billy handed Holmes Jackson's tits. She pulled out first one side of his shirt, then the other, while he fitted them over his chest. Then she uncapped her lipstick. 'Go like this.' Holmes tilted his face to her, lips peeled open, watching her eyes flicker from one cosmetic detail to the next. Eyes like black candles; the iris floating on the white like a lily on a light-sealed pond. When he was alone, Holmes spent hours in the mirror trying to make his eyes bulge like Billy's. Close up, under the neon, Holmes saw the skin underneath Billy's eyes was bruised like his mother's after she'd been crying. When Billy mascaraed his sandy lashes, his eyes darkened to the blue of a winter ocean. Then Jackson and Billy set upon Holmes' hair, wetting it, teasing it. Jackson said he looked like Doris Day on a bad hair day. They gave Jackson a Mandy, had one themselves, then spilt out of the toilets laughing. Billy cloaked her skirt.

The barman wasn't sure about Billy: she didn't quite fit the bill. So Holmes got the drinks and they built towers on their table with the empty glasses. A safe sex evangelist dropped condoms on their table and Holmes began to blow them up and pop them. Then Billy disappeared and Holmes was dancing with Jackson, the inflatable tits flying through the air between them, bouncing off the other dancers.

Jackson's face wide open with laughter, Holmes went down on the back of the dancefloor, then he was outside, throwing up in the gutter, a hand on the back of his neck, stroking him, soothing him. He remembered the man's bedroom ceiling—a parachute silk—and the constant negotiations. The man had been infected with that fear, wouldn't let Holmes fuck him, could only come with his own hand. Holmes stood out of the morning sunlight and drank two schooners of water while the man's cat wrapped itself around his legs, mewing and purring. He left the house without waking the man. The punks lined the wall in front of Paddington markets like so many parrots. Spinifex hair, all those lurid colours of the cocktails he had drunk the night before, he turned down a back street and vomited quietly between two parked cars.

Holmes was coming up Oxford Street. Behind the buildings in the east, an eruption of white and grey cumulus in the humid blue sky. Holmes wiped his brow in the window of the furniture shop, and saw the faint maculation of healing blisters around his hairline. When Billy had cut his hair she found the roots so dark she had to peroxide it twice. The bleach burnt and she soothed his skin with fingertips dipped in cool milk. Discount washing machines and chairs roped one to the other, Holmes thought of Warren each time he passed the shop, how Warren had looked at him, long and hard, when Holmes was there last week. Holmes knew this white tufted hair made him an angel, sullied, large-eyed and wan. His mother in the bathroom yelling over the scream of the hair-dryer to Holmes in the kitchen who stood at the open fridge, eating leftovers. Warren twisted in the lounge-room chair to see him better while Holmes' mother kept talking. 'Warren and I are going to the drive-in tonight, Pete darling. You're welcome to join us.' Holmes had seen how the skin now sagged along her upper arms. He cocked his hip and let Warren the Rat get a good look at what he was missing out on. In your dreams, Ratface. 'No thanks Mum.'

Holmes had quickly become fluent in this subterranean language, all day every day cruising in full view of impervious heterosexuals. Delighting in the novelty of this new syntax, he talked for the sake of it, he attracted more comments than he could answer, more requests than he could fulfil. Fielded them on buses and trains, in streets and supermarkets. The other day he had sex in a car; the day after in the toilets at Bondi Pavilion. Last week he got picked up in a milk bar and taken home to the boyfriend for a threesome. He got a different sort of trade in this get-up: not so crusty; younger, more hip. He had noticed two women doing it at Central Station last week, and this had shocked him then thrilled him. Another one who wanted him—the son of the owner of the Lebanese takeaway. Holmes strutted. The world was his oyster. He put a Winfield in his mouth, and smelt apple shampoo beneath his fingernails.

If he was ever in love it was with Matt the Peacock. The Peacock used to put cochineal in his hair—green and blue, sometimes red. He was the best skateboarder in Seaforth: 360s, handstands, you name it. After the swimming carnival they went for a surf then Holmes stayed the night. His saltiness, and the sea, and the chlorine. That was years ago, when they were twelve, maybe thirteen. The next morning they washed each other's hair with apple shampoo, a cochineal rainbow pooling around their feet. The Peacock already had a deep voice and heaps of hair; Holmes remembered it against the palm of his hand, resistant. Soft, yet resistant. They were best friends until Natalie came along. Natalie Slobovich, or something like that. Natalie

Slutofabitch was what Holmes called her, as he told Billy the day she brought home a sheaf of peacock feathers to use in a headdress. She groaned at Natalie's nickname then said, 'You know how peacock's make their tail feathers?'

'How?'

'By eating thorns.'

'I'm sick of covering up for you, Peter.' Lizzie was cleaning the living room. 'Mum's on the phone practically every day, you know. She told me you'd got the sack from the news-agency.'

Holmes lifted his legs for his sister to vacuum beneath them. They were long, lean and pale, a fine scar down one thigh where a fin had gashed him in Year Nine. A bush of dark yellow hibiscus grew close to the window behind him, pushing its flowers against the glass like handfuls of limp crepe. Holmes said he wasn't going back to school, he said he was moving out and Lizzie scoffed he wasn't old enough to sign a lease. Holmes thought of Billy, there was no one else he could live with but she had no room. Holmes knew then that he was alone.

He watched his childhood drift away as his sister plunged the vacuum behind the bursting cushions of the old couch. He felt helpless, resentful and an anger surfaced that he knew he would need to keep living. Lizzie said their mother had a right to worry, she knew as well as Lizzie did what Holmes was, what he was getting into. Lizzie said Holmes had chosen a difficult path and maybe, just maybe, he was burning his bridges because maybe their mother wouldn't have him back even if he wanted to go and really, Lizzie couldn't blame her. She said it would be best if he left that day.

Holmes pleaded with Billy to teach him how to blast. They did speed, speedballs if they had more money. They took gear out with them and topped up in the toilets, gripping each other's arms above the elbow, sometimes lighting a match to see. At Stranded when the taps were dry, Billy flushed the toilet and filled the lid of her lipstick under the clean jet of water, then they cooked the speed in a chocolate foil licked clean by Holmes. The music pumped through to them and Holmes leant against the door, shutting his eyes as the rush escalated his spine, gripped his throat. He saw the horn section burst up an arpeggio like flowers on a vine opening one after the other, spilling their colours down his eyelids. He felt Billy's hand on his cheek and opened his eyes to find her staring at him strangely. 'Gee you look beautiful when you're out of it.' Then she recapped the syringe and slid it into the pencil pocket on the thigh of her army pants. 'You right, Homie?' she cocked her head. 'Okay now? Shall we go?' She left the toilet and he followed her out. White nights, wild nights, they danced till Stranded closed then kept on dancing to Grace Jones at Billy's Darlinghurst Road studio while the sky lightened outside the window.

'Hey Billy, you home?'

Her door is a ajar and Holmes can see the television screen in the corner, the newsreader's tie poking like a garish wildflower through the dull grey fields of his double-breasted jacket. Holmes knows Billy is expecting him. He shuts the door but doesn't move forward. The studio is now full of the scent of mangoes, spiriting to him a host of other summer luxuries: long beach days, new wetsuits, north coast holiday. He craves the taste but no mangoes are visible. Holmes knows the skin or sucked seed could be buried anywhere. For a cleaner Billy's pretty dirty. The place is even worse than last week. A pile of clothes, suitcases, shoes, materials looming out of the bed alcove; the fold-out couch folded out, spilt muesli caked in a crevice of the sheet; everything you can think of on the floor—belts, junk mail, ashtrays, used fits—and over the doorway to the kitchenette crammed with a desk and chair, all the way around from one wall to the one opposite, a thick electrical cord held in place with gaffa, leading to the power pack for Billy's sewing machine, record player and television.

Holmes looks down over William Street. A hush of night is drawing over from the east. He can see the Harbour Bridge lit green, the fractured geometry of office buildings, the beginning of the Cahill Expressway. After a southerly buster each city light is clear and fresh beneath the intense black sky. It excites him, the movement of carlights, the neon line and clacking of a train emerging then disappearing, the nasal nee-naw of sirens drifting into him. Then a clattering of boots on the metal walkway between this and the building adjacent: Billy coming back from her dealer.

'I can pay, you know.'

'Where'd you get it, Homie?'

'What?'

'The money.'

Holmes shuffles through the steps of 'YMCA', face to the window. 'Hey Billy, d'you wanna clone tonight?' he turns.

'Doing tricks now, are we?' Billy stands there, hands on hips. Her collar is turned up and held with a shoelace tie, nickel cow skull touching her throat, not quite hiding a long narrow hickey.

'What's that?' Homes just his chin forward.

'Mozzie bit me. I hope you're doing it safe, Holmes.'

'Why? Are you? Where'd you get that love bite? Who did it? Tell me, Billy.'

'I don't really have to be safe. I picked up last night.'

'Why should I be safe if you aren't? Where'd you go? I looked for you everywhere.' Holmes paces around, sits edgily on the bed. 'Who were you with? It's not fair, Billy, I tell you everything.'

Billy flops onto the bed next to him. 'Poor baby. I'll tell you all about her if you're a good boy.'

'Don't patronise me!' Homes takes the last cigarette then flings the packet across the room. A coldness comes over him, nausea. It's not just last night; Billy has been doing this all along. The cigarettes here the other day—they weren't her brand. The bruises around her arm last week. How she disappeared at Patches that night; the girl at the Love Bomb Disco crouching to spin the egg-timer in Billy's timezone suit. Holmes takes Billy's lighter then turns away from her. 'Come on Homer, why so angry?' Billy's arms creep around his waist. 'Aren't I allowed to have a sex life?'

'Course you are. But why d'you have to be so secretive?'

'I'm not. It's just that you never asked before.'

'I don't wanna know anyway,' Holmes mutters, drawing his legs up, hugging them. Billy's sigh falls across the back of his neck and he shivers. 'There was a king tide today,' she runs her hand through his hair. 'The jetty at Elizabeth Bay was almost underwater. It was incredible. Apparently people were even surfing at some of the harbour beaches, that one opposite the Heads, Chowder something. And a fisherman got washed off at Bronte.'

Giddy with cigarettes, humidity and her dark sexuality, Holmes lies back and covers his face. He remembers a childhood dream: sunrise over the harbour, a swell coming through the Heads; the waves roll in, pipes under silk. He is paddling out from Manly Cove, out to the open ocean to mount the bombora, leaning into the wave and surfing all the way across to Port Jackson. And as the wave dies beneath him near the brown rocks of Pinchgut, he turns to a suddenly darkened harbour, wall of water rearing behind the Heads, all along the coast, swallowing the sun.

'I used to have nightmares when there were king tides,' he says. 'I used to think there'd be a tidal wave.' He feels the mattress rise beside him and hears the rustle of Billy changing her clothes. 'I'm boiling,' she says. When he pulls the sheet away, Billy is wearing the man's dinner shirt that he bought her from a Kings Cross op shop. He counted the fine pleats across the chest as he walked back to her place—fourteen on either side. The top is slightly open, the cuffs hang down over her hands and the tails halfway down her thighs. She goes to the fridge for a beer and Holmes watches her bending, the shirt lifting to reveal the smooth insides of her thighs, the dark crevice at the top. He realises he is hard and buries his face in the pillow, trying not to cry.

Holmes left Billy waiting at the gate while he went inside his sister's house to collect his surfboard. He had walked the streets for hours, obsessed with a desire to see the ocean, then woken Billy at seven, dragged her out of bed. He knew she was still cross with him and so took the last pieces of Toblerone from Lizzie's fridge as a peace offering. It had rained before dawn and steam rose from the back streets of Paddington. Sweet, sticky smell of frangipanis beaten to a paste along the footpath, dropping from the trees as Billy and Holmes trudged up the hill, Billy not talking.

Holmes knew this wind would bring up the ocean, full moon last night, and that the tide would be right for the banks at Bondi. He wanted Billy to see it as though he'd invented it, but she didn't forgive him until the bus reached the end of Bondi Road and the ocean was before them, glimmering in the sun. White waves peaked all the way out to the horizon and Holmes scuffed the sand to where the rain hadn't penetrated then spread his towel for Billy to sit on.

The surf was big and Holmes got dumped the first time he paddled out. The second time he got dumped he emerged gasping to see Billy on the beach, waving vigorously. He turned to the sun and paddled again, sure she was laughing. There was a lull and he got out the back where he lay for a while, resting his cheek on one hand, letting the other drift alongside in the warm water.

It wasn't until he took off that he realised how big the wave really was. Dark mouth yawning below he whimpered with fear and for a split second he saw her there, sitting bolt upright. He drove up the wave and did a re-entry, Billy's face coming closer, white round and still, then he plummeted with the hiss of the lip furling behind him, around him, enclosing him. And inside the thunder Holmes hunched forward, waiting for the aperture, waiting for air.

IN THE FOREST OF
THE ETERNALS

LOUIS NOWRA

He was lost in the fog. He paused on the footpath under a tree with no leaves. Should he go left or right? The fog had descended quickly and, immersed in his thoughts, he was unaware of how thick it had become until he found himself at a corner unable to read the street sign. A dull rattle emerged from the murk and a car suddenly, noisily, appeared and then abruptly vanished. Somewhere nearby there was the lonely clop clop of a horse in careful steady gait. Then it was gone and everything was silent again.

He sighed. If he retraced his steps it would be only fifteen minutes before he was back in his Hotel Cecil bedroom. But he had been in bed all day and the more he stayed in bed, the more a sense of paralysis gripped him. He lifted his head to gaze at the bare boughs. In Australia it was day and the sky would be clear, bright, explicable. He shivered as a momentary wave of chill raced through his coat into the very marrow of his bones.

The lassitude that had possessed him in the hotel room was still with him, making him incapable of even deciding which street to take. He had a mental map of London, especially this part of the city, but if he chose the wrong street in this exasperating miasma then even he would soon be lost. Time to make a decision, he told himself and, with a shrug, he headed down the street to his left.

He passed down a street of terrace houses. Almost within touching distance were vertical lines of dull yellow light trying to escape into the fog through the cracks in drawn curtains. Inside those rooms were men home from work, secure in their certainties, and wives, calm, placid wives, instructing their servants and nannies. His own wife was in the country with Lady Montswell. Pattie had reluctantly accompanied him to England and, because she was worried by his melancholy, had just as reluctantly gone on a short holiday.

The public orator, the man of indefatigable energy, was nowhere to be seen in private. It was as if the more energy he spent on others, the more spectral he had become in Pattie's presence. But after years of marriage she knew not to question him. Instead she knew he should be allowed to withdraw into himself like some dark heavy stone of introspection sinking into the dark lake of his unconsciousness. His inner self had always been hidden from everyone, including his own wife.

Sometimes, when the marriage was young, she had wanted to peek at his journals. She had wanted him to share his thoughts with her and was irritated at being locked out from a significant part of him but he kept them under lock and key. Perhaps, as she had fretted as a young bride, the journals contained remarks about her, but now, after three decades, she supposed they were probably only about himself. She had come to the middle-aged conclusion that of all the men she had known, he was the most preoccupied with his own thoughts, his own musings, his own massive doubts. If once she had been anxious about what the journals said about her, she now disliked them because they provoked his introspection. Each new blank page sucked him into its snowy vortex of self-absorption. Yet, she did love him. That was certain and sure. At the constant round of receptions they were seldom together, as they were separated by the rituals of formal occasions, but his eyes would seek her out across a room and when they found her they seemed to be saying, 'Are you all right?' She would smile reassuringly, then turn her attention back to the inane, shrill chatter of society matrons.

There was the muffled sound of raucous laughter coming from a house within touching distance. He paused. It had that obscene full-throated sound of men in a room without women. Perhaps they were part of his negotiating team . . . perhaps not. More likely his team was still at the Hotel Cecil, drinking themselves into boisterous spirits before they caroused away the night at some gentleman's club and music hall. In previous visits to London, he had always asked for a hotel far away from his entourage, but he had given in this time, given in to the tedium of forced bonhomie.

The six weeks in London had been a frenzy of faces and names. There had been fifty formal luncheons and dinners and he had made fifty speeches. There had been receptions, meetings, and weekends at great houses—the English did things like that very well. They were a nation of brilliant gestures. For six weeks he had spent less than four or five hours in bed a night. He rose early to read documents and letters in order to prepare for the gruelling day ahead. There had been fifteen days at the Imperial Conference, where he had felt the full weight on him, a burden that Botha, the South African Prime Minister, did not have to carry because his English was so bad. The slothful French–Canadian Prime Minister, Laurier, didn't care. It had been up to him to provide a vision. But now the view was clouded. Many things were clouded. Maybe the fog that had descended on the city was a cataract forming over his once-grand vision.

In a moment of exasperation he had given his book on irrigation to the Boer, who even after his translator had explained its title and theme, still had not understood its significance. South Africa had a climate like Australia and that asinine, grinning, muddle-headed Botha did not comprehend what was being said to him. Australia had achieved an agricultural paradise, a golden sea of wheat that was going to drown the world markets and inaugurate a dazzling age of Austral prosperity. He hated to think badly of people, but the Boer's obtuseness so irritated him that he had to stop himself from shouting him down.

Figures emerged from the fog; a couple, a young couple arm in arm. They almost collided with him. The man apologised, the woman giggled. Then they were gone before he had a chance to ask if he were on the right street. The English had changed since he were last in London: men were corpulent, the women had become plain and ashen faced, the old women were flabby and shapeless. Fatness was a sure sign of immoderation. At the dinners and receptions he had been appalled by the amount everyone ate and drank. At one luncheon he had been unable to touch his food. He was overwhelmed by the enormous piece of meat swimming in the fatty gravy before him and, gazing over at the assembled diners, he saw not men and women, but sections of them, as if the men and women had been replaced by plump cheeks, greasy chins, fat-stained moustaches, parsley-stained teeth, bubble lips, hanging chins, swollen cheeks, dribbling mouths, corpulent tongues. When he had stood up at the end of the dinner to deliver his speech he could not look at any individual, because there were none left. He saw only mounds of gluttonous, insensate flesh before him.

The memory of that occasion made him shudder and he stopped in mid-step, puzzled as to why he had reacted so strongly to a sight he had seen many times, countless times, before. He did not want to feel repulsed by people, but they had disgustingly violated their bodies. Their insatiability was naked and unapologetic. Perhaps he was more conscious of bodies because his own body was extremely tense and had been since the first day he and Pattie had set sail for England. They had left Adelaide on March 7, but his bowels had remained tight for two days, until, after much effort, he had had his first 'skip'. Then there was the ptomaine poisoning on arriving in April. For the past five days the deep-breathing exercises and concentration had not helped him to evacuate. Five days of insomnia, worry and the inability to rid himself of the toxic contents of his bowels, had nearly driven him to distraction.

He knew the reason for this. Five days before, standing in that room of oafish greed, he had faltered during his speech. Even during his first visit to London, years before, consumed as he was by nervous apprehension, he had never faltered, even when speaking, as he generally did, extemporaneously, surprising the English who had underestimated this 'colonial'. His reputation was enhanced as it had been in Australia by the fact that his speeches were delivered without notes, without hesitation. To falter in a search for the right word had been a nightmarish experience. Eventually he found the exact word he had been looking for, but it had been a bewildering journey of sounds looking for meaning. He knew the word he wanted to say, that is, its sounds, but even on mentally hearing the sounds it didn't provide him with a visual image of the word. It was as if he had been standing on a railway platform, enveloped in the rising clouds of steam, his ears inundated with the sound of hissing, his eyes frustrated at being unable to see the make of the train engine. As he peered into the dense vapour he felt perspiration dribbling from his armpits and, panic-stricken, had said the first word that came into his mind. It propelled him back in the flow of the speech and, thankfully, sounds and meaning coalesced into order and harmony again. The falter had been momentary, but for him, it had been an eternity. At the end of his speech, he nodded his thanks at the applause, but his mind had backtracked to that gap in his memory—what was the word he had said and what was its meaning?

He had left the luncheon in a daze of introspection and in the foyer accidentally bumped into the doorman, who, like a rubber man, bounced off the wall and bumped up against an astonished middle-aged woman. Instead of concern, he found himself laughing. The woman was appalled as were the witnesses but he didn't notice, it was as if the incident had happened on a stage and he was watching it from the front stalls of some ornate theatre. He left the hotel and, refusing to take a carriage, walked back to the Cecil with Pattie. By arrival, he had convinced himself that the forgotten word had been a momentary aberration.

Yet the following day, as he sat like some naive student before his favourite novelist, George Meredith, now an invalid near death, he found himself unable to remember the title of Meredith's most famous novel. In his mind's eye he could see a list of Meredith's published work but the title he was searching for was not on it. He had wanted to praise him, tell him that this novel had meant everything to him as a youth, but how could he praise Meredith if he couldn't even recall the name of the book?

He did not sleep that night, but tossed and turned in an agonisingly futile attempt to discover the reason for his increasing forgetfulness. Perhaps it was the painful carbuncles that had spread across his chest and buttocks? Perhaps the strain of the Imperial Conference. The pressure of all those meetings, speeches, dinners, people. Perhaps it was those things plus the cumulation of thirty years of public life, the difficulties of being Prime Minister in a rowdy, juvenile nation, the struggle for Federation, for irrigation, for the defence of Australia as the last bastion of the Anglo-Saxon race.

Next morning he spent several hours with Tweedmouth, the First Lord of the Admiralty. On the way there, his carriage following a few paces behind him on the roadside, the cockney driver mystified at this colonial's habit of walking everywhere, a car nearly ran down an ancient woman with a bent back who was crossing the street, oblivious to the new motorised vehicles. The car swerved, just missing her, hit the footpath, and bounced past him barely a yard away, and crashed into a stone fence. He helped the unhurt driver from the car. 'That was lucky,' said the driver as they both stared at the crumpled front of the car. He nodded, believing that Fate had not deemed him to die yet. If it were a sign that he was to be spared, then what was the purpose of being spared?

Tweedmouth was charming and well-mannered, and spoke in that cooing, soothing fashion that the English upper class reserved for interesting colonials. 'O,' he said with lips that perfectly formed a round entrance into the slimy pink interior of his mouth, 'we know Australia wants a special relationship with Britain and yet it is hard to reconcile the two points of your agenda, Prime Minister, in that you want a special relationship with us, the Mother Country, by wanting us to buy your wheat and your wool, despite the fact that we can buy it cheaper elsewhere. And yet, and I stress the yet, and please do not misunderstand, Prime Minister, and yet you want your own navy, which is like saying you do not think we can protect you, and I know you are not saying that, but you do seem to be underestimating the potency of the British navy, and therefore the

British nation as a whole, and, and, and, (he paused, bouncing on the trampoline of the conjunction, grasping for a polite way of expressing himself) you must understand that although you are some 12 000 miles away, our navy rules the Indian ocean and the danger of our navy being caught unawares especially by the Japanese, who you seem to fear, is, I assure you, quite minimal.'

The words began to resemble a cat's soothing purr. They had no meaning, only a tranquillising effect and for a brief hallucinatory, frightening moment, he saw Tweedmouth curled up before a fireplace, purring softly, smiling broadly, his body gradually vanishing into the soft darkness of shadows cast by the fire until only his radiant grin was left. Peering more closely, he was disturbed by sight of the teeth transforming themselves into the terrifying knife-like incisors of some large feline predator, with clumps of putrefying meat lodged between the blood-stained molars.

Tweedmouth must have noticed the shocked, pale face, because he stopped and asked the Prime Minister if he had said anything offensive. The Prime Minister shook his head, indicating no, but also tried to shake his head free of the hallucination. He wanted to tell Tweedmouth that he was, like every Australian, a British patriot and that he was in no, no way, criticising the preparedness of the navy but did *he* not understand that Australia was in Asia and the Japanese had recently defeated the Russian navy? Australia was vulnerable. It needed its own navy to protect itself from the swarming hordes of Asiatics.

That's what he wanted to say but didn't, given the fact he had little idea what Tweedmouth was talking about. Taking silence as consent, Tweedmouth continued to purr, while the Prime Minister covertly counted the number of steps he would have to take in order to leave the room. Eleven, perhaps twelve, to reach the door, and beyond the door was fresh air to clear his head of its bafflement. Eventually Tweedmouth stopped and, pleading a pressing appointment, the Prime Minister almost leapt out of his chair walked ten large steps to the door. In the street he loudly breathed in and out, trying to suck in as much air as possible, enough to stop him from fainting with fatigue and the horror of what he had just experienced. His carriage driver was surprised to see him signal to be driven back to the hotel.

On the way back to the Hotel Cecil he had made a decision. It was this decision that explained why he was in the fog hoping he was now in Astor Street. He spotted a house number. Unable to read it he walked up the steps and saw the number 24. He moved on to the next house and found himself at 22, the number he had been seeking—that is if he were indeed in Astor Street and wasn't lost. He knocked on the door. His beard and hair were lank with moisture, his body cold. The door half opened and a maid appeared, slightly puzzled to see this gaunt, tall man standing before her.

'What can I do for you, sir?'

'I've come to see Mrs Morrison. My name is Alfred Deakin.'

On hearing his name the maid smiled, gave a slight bow and opened the door fully.

The entrance hall was warm and comfortable with a wall table vase full of peacock feathers and a Persian hall runner richly coloured with dark blues, crimsons and yellows. He felt immediately at ease. His apprehensions about the visit vanished. The maid took his coat and asked him to follow her into the sitting room.

He sat on a canary-yellow chaise longue. The walls were papered with a blue and white design of angel trumpet flowers and above the black marble fireplace was a large framed photograph. He recognised the face of Madame Blavatsky, the founder of Theosophy. Her face resembled a bland bun studded with two black opals. Ever since he had seen her picture in a book frontispiece several decades before, it had always been with a sense of bemusement that he had contemplated her countenance. How had such a coarse body become the vessel for such a refined spiritual mind? At first he had many reservations about her and when she had written about transportation he had decided to test her theories. He and several friends had sat in a dark, hermetically-sealed seance room and, after calling up a spirit and asking it to transport any object from nearby St Kilda beach had, after half an hour, turned on the lights to find the floor littered with kelp, shells, starfish and dozens of grotesque sea insectivores writhing helplessly on the carpet.

His thoughts were interrupted by Mrs Morrison's arrival. 'Alfred, how are you?' she said from the doorway. He stood up and smiled, slightly disappointed. He had not seen her for some fifteen years and, like Madame Blavatsky, she had grown podgy. The blowzy coarseness of her face was muted by the soft pompadour hair style. Once she had been only plumpish but her small figure had ballooned out and her breasts, made even more exaggerated by the loose-fitting silk blouse, were enormous.

They shook hands. Her hand was warm and moist, his cold and dry. He had not changed; still that ramrod-straight figure, the Van Dyke beard, rather long, oval-shaped head and light baritone voice. Obviously he had kept, as ever, to his abstemious habits. It was his eyes that were different. She remembered them as being scintillating, incandescent; now there was something opaque about them, as if they were glazed by some inner pain.

'I have everything prepared,' she said, but realising he was over-anxious to begin and, therefore, was in an appropriate mood, she asked him to have tea with her. As he sipped tea in his familiar staccato fashion, she talked of how pleased she was to see his name in the English newspapers. 'After all,' she said proudly, 'I predicted you would marry an auburn-haired girl and that you would become Prime Minister.' That was years before, before she returned to England to continue her career as a spiritualist.

.Back in England she had immersed herself even more—if that were possible—into the world of theosophy, spiritualism and the afterlife. Deakin, however, if not renouncing spiritualism, had let it become secondary to his life, something that disappointed Mrs Morrison who had regarded him as one of the most promising spiritualists she had ever encountered. At his first attempt at hypnosis he had made a girl swoon helplessly into his arms. His astonished expression at his success had made her laugh out loud.

As they spoke about various things, Deakin jumped from topic to topic and Mrs Morrison realised that he seemed to be possessed by a peculiar agitation. She tried to make light of his lessening interest in spiritualism, telling him that she still regarded him as the medium he once was, but instead of being a conduit for the voices of the dead, he was now a medium for the Australian people. Instead of accepting what she had said as a compliment he moaned slightly. 'If I am, then I am losing that ability, Mrs Morrison. Me afraid that I may be speaking from inside a kind of darkness.'

The curious turn of phrase and his abject shrug unnerved Mrs Morrison. She gave him a comforting pat on his hand and called for her maid, who returned with a brown paper parcel. 'We should begin as soon as possible, Alfred,' she smiled, telling him she would return in fifteen minutes. She left the sitting room, closing the door behind her and instructed the maid to go to her room and only come when called.

Alone in the sitting room Alfred, with trembling fingers, fumbled with the string. He took a deep breath and told himself to be calm. With a few sure movements of his momentarily steady hands he unwrapped the parcel. He lifted up the velvet material. Holding it before him with outstretched hands, it tumbled open. Before him was a pale purple dress. The bosom was a billowing cloud of velvet and lace. The dress tapered in at the waist and ran smoothly over the hips and, with a minimum of fullness, to the knees. Then it flared outwards in a frothy grandeur of cream lace and ruffles which poured out into a bell-shape that would slightly drift behind the wearer, as if the dress were a frozen mauve waterfall ending in a mist of white water.

When Mrs Morrison returned he was dressed. The gown was too large for his gaunt figure and he resembled a scarecrow. He looked unsure and she smiled reassuringly. 'Purple is the most spiritual colour, as you know.' He stood in deep thought as Mrs Morrison cleared the large oak table. Of all the men she had known he was the most solitary—even in company, when seeming to enjoy himself, there was an air of apartness, even loneliness, about him, a curious remoteness, as if he were viewing people through an opaque window.

She lit a candle and turned off the lights. They sat at opposite ends of the table, their faces flickering with yellow light and shadows. Mrs Morrison was the finest medium he had ever met. Her insistence that he wear a dress for important seances was something he had quickly agreed to because he intuitively knew that he had to become two in order to become one. He had to become both man and woman in order to become both and, at the same time, rise above just being either male or female. A man in a dress was neither sex, and therefore an asexual and single spiritual entity.

'What do you wish to enquire about, Alfred?'

'Something is happening to me and I don't know what it is,' he said in a curiously hesitant voice.

'With whom of the Eternals do you wish to speak?'

'J.S. Mill,' he said quietly.

She closed her eyes and spoke to the dead. A few moments later her body shuddered, as if something were trying to erupt from inside her. She became a vessel empty of her own self. Her voice changed, growing deeper, as she became a conduit for J.S. Mill. The English philosopher remembered Deakin and was pleased to speak to him again, asking him what he wanted to know. 'Me afflicted at last with a sense of a wasted life. Me shallow and poor and frail in spirit and mind and flesh. Me selfish and barren. Me humiliated. Me shamed.'

'But what is it you want to know?' asked the baritone voice emerging from Mrs Morrison's throat.

'I don't know. I was hoping you'd tell me.'

There was a silence and for a few moments Deakin thought that Mrs Morrison had gone to sleep, but then the soothing voice returned. 'I'm afraid, Alfred, I can't see anything in front of me. Or you. It's as if I'm blind. This is a very strange sensation.'

Deakin cross-questioned him but the brilliant Eternal was, uniquely, at a loss for words.

When called up, Socrates, like Mill, was ambiguous: 'You will be in darkness before the final darkness.'

'It is something personal you are after, isn't it, Alfred?' asked Mrs Morrison.

'I think it is,' he said, confused by his own questions.

He asked Mrs Morrison to call up Giordano Bruno, the hermetic scientist who had died at the stake not recanting his belief that the earth revolved around the sun. 'What is happening to me?' Deakin asked. Said the soft tenor voice: 'Finish your job and turn in.'

It was well after midnight when an exhausted Mrs Morrison opened her eyes. 'I don't have the energy to call up any more Eternals.' Deakin nodded. He was exhausted too, but more than that, he was frightened. Mrs Morrison saw black rivulets slowly working their way out of his nostrils and down his philtrum. She turned on the lights and saw it was blood. 'Alfred, you have a bloody nose.' He sat upright, looking into the distance, not aware of it or aware of Mrs Morrison wiping away the blood. She put the handkerchief in his hand and, as if manipulating a doll, lifted up his arm. Automatically he held the handkerchief against his nose and allowed her to guide him to the chaise longue where he lay down. 'I think you should rest here for a time,' she said. He nodded slightly and closed his eyes.

In the darkness of his closed eyes, the words of the Eternals whirled around, like some willy-willy spinning itself across a featureless desert. What did they mean? There was no answer, just an enervating sense of hopelessness. He felt as if a darkness was closing in on him, a darkness that even the Eternals could not explain. Perhaps the Eternals didn't have a word for such a darkness?

In the morning the maid was startled to see the guest wearing a dress and asleep on the chaise longue. By the time Mrs Morrison had risen, Deakin was awake. He thanked her for the seance and said it had helped, but she could tell by the dark rings under his eyes and the agitated manner that it hadn't. He changed back into his suit and before going Mrs Morrison wrapped up the dress and gave it to him. 'You may need this to call up the Eternals again,' she said. He was reluctant to take the parcel but she was insistent. Maybe in Australia, the Eternals would be more specific and then they could help this lost man.

Deakin woke from a dream that he was on a ship heading back to Australia, then realised he was. A curtain covered the two portholes of his deluxe cabin. Across from him, in the other bed, Pattie slept soundlessly. Deakin got out of bed and peeked through a curtain. It was night and beyond the dark sea was a horizon of a billion bright stars. He dressed, quickly and silently as possible, and then took a brown package from one of his suitcases.

The ship was quiet. Everyone seemed to be asleep as he moved along the main deck and then under the poop deck to the stern where the ensign fluttered lightly in the warm Indian Ocean breeze. He looked at the full moon casting white light on the frosty waves of the churning water left in the ship's wake. The world was still and peaceful and he wished he could be the same. But since he had boarded the ship he had come to the realisation that England had been one of his greatest failures. The British had not listened to him, and his desire for Australia to have its own navy was thought to be anti-British.

When he thought back on those six weeks it seemed as though he had lived through an insurrection. a constant night-time attack in dank, impenetrable mist. Earlier that evening as he dressed for dinner he had looked at himself in the mirror and had seen defeat. Next to that weary face was a reflection of the bedside table and on it was a copy of Meredith's *The Egoist* which he had been attempting to read, despite the annoying lapses in his concentration. He had read it some dozen times during his life and he was stunned to realise he had forgotten most of it. Not only had the title slipped his mind when talking to the author, but he had forgotten main characters and the story itself.

Is that how he would end up, propped up in an invalid chair, a shrivelled parody of his former self? In a fit of irritation, he grabbed the book, opened the porthole and cast his favourite novel into the seas.

Reflecting on that uncharacteristic action he realised he had become a man utterly unlike the title. He had no ego because his self was vanishing. Deep in the forest of increasing shadows and gloom, he was even forgetting himself. Now he understood what the Eternals were saying: ahead of him lay darkness before he died. He would live out the final years God had granted him in a darkening mental oblivion, an oblivion that didn't have the dark energy of madness, but one that had the ennui and inertia of a weary, exhausted brain. As he gazed at the agitated water streaming brightly from the stern he smiled to himself. He remembered the word he had faltered on—water! Yes, he had been talking about irrigating those golden Austral plains of wheat and when he searched for the word water he found a blank. And it was a blank because the word water no longer held its potency. He had spent so much time convincing Australians about irrigation that he was drained of enthusiasm. He was like a puppet bouncing around a stage, his limbs jiggled by the strings of stale rhetoric.

He opened the package and took out the dress, running his fingers across the hushed velvet. There was no point in keeping it. The Eternals would only tell him the same thing in other seances. It occurred to him that perhaps the only times of true happiness were when he had worn dresses to communicate with the Eternals. In a dress he felt he had lost his flesh and become a spirit himself, beyond sex, body, ego and temptation.

With a sharp grunt of effort he threw the dress into the sea. It drifted a little in the breeze and landed in the bubbling foam, bouncing anxiously as if it were a woman who now regretted having jumped from the ship, and then, resigned, sank beneath the luminous waves into the nocturnal depths. The urge to join the dress was almost too much and Deakin clutched the guard rail violently, sucking in deep gasping breaths, trying to stop himself from jumping.

A woman with long unruly hair was leaning back against the hand rail as a bearded man kissed her passionately. On hearing footsteps they turned, startled to see a thin silhouetted figure passing by. 'I thought it was a ghost,' giggled the woman. Deakin paid no attention to the couple as he walked slowly through the moonlit shadows of the main deck. He knew now what the future had in store for him. He would die twice. The encroaching mental darkness would be the first death and the eventual death of his body would be his second and final death. He bent his head as he climbed through the hatch and descended into the twilight of the lower deck corridors.

VENICE—THE ARIA

DOROTHY PORTER

Bring me my mask of burning gold
Bring me my canal of fire . . .

Tonight
  it's Sleaze Ball
with techno-funk grinding
  in my chest
    like a chisel

I'm staggering
    not dancing

sweat crawls
    under my wig
    like lice

there is no disguise
      like misery
I know everyone
no one knows me

Tonight
    I'm not sparkles

I'm all squint
where's Nicky?

the boys smoke and glitter
the boys don't see me at all

I titter and totter
    too tall for these heels

Oh, Nicky, we never went
    to Venice

we never cruised the Carnival
    in murky masks
we never fell
    in the Grand Canal

my honey-pot, my hungry boy
    love is as ancient
    as flood and excess

on love
    we float like rot

Oh, we were too fastidious
    we picked over each other's
        twitching faces
            for fleas

we stopped itching
        and lost

we never picked over
    that flooded glory city

So now
  your hygienic queen
howls
  behind dry make-up
desolate
  as rayon

who will hold
  this gaudy fussy hand?

what stinky wind
  off still water
do you sniff and forget?

Let me be a Big Girl
    a Brave Girl
forsake
    this blubbering tizz

does this anguish
  demand an audience
    like leaky silicon breasts?

Nicky, there is a city
    called Venice

not a New Age Atlantis
  festooned with kelp
    and wishful thinking

there is a city
  called Venice

struggling under

its own swamps
and rubbish

smelly and magnificent

like love in the mortal flesh.

TOTTERING TOWARDS DARLINGHURST

GARY DUNNE

I like riding in a stretch limo. Like cocaine, it's something I knew I'd like even before the first taste. By the time we reach the end of my street, I'm hooked. It's so roomy, all reeking of luxury and chemical freshness.

I suspect tonight is the first time for all of us. I'm only sitting here because I'm escorting The Big W to this drag gala awards night. She's heard she's likely to be presented with something or other for centuries of service, both on stage and in the epidemic's frontline. It was her idea that I come. She's been at me for months to get out more often.

We are both dressed to die for. I'm in Commes des Garçons. Over a year ago I inherited a whole up-market wardrobe that fits perfectly. Unfortunately much of it makes me look like Elton John.

The Big W is in a relatively simple, timeless, beige creation off-set by a modest excess of jewellery, some of which may actually be real. It's her medium-budget glam ensemble, perfect, she says, for a community icon at the height of her career.

She pops the first champagne cork. We toast each other and life in general. I try to guess her age and realise that she's looked over thirty-five for as long as I've known her. We met back in the 1970s when I was a teenage fan and she was one of Caps' more frequent transvestite glamour stars, known simply as Ms Margaret Whitlam. She's slimmer now, still as tall as ever and still capable of intimidating anything from a modest dinner party to a drunken rabble in a nightclub. She's my oldest friend, a label she doesn't mind as much as she used to. These days I'm probably her oldest friend as well.

Our first stop is to pick up Lauren, her diminutive sidekick, who, as predicted, has teamed black with black. Tonight's outfit has a post-apocalyptic edge, a result of the layers of black hessian and black leather she has appliquéd together like papier-mâché. Retro-gothic makeup, a jet-black hair-do, thick stockings and boots complete the picture.

Lauren has always been her own creation. Even as a teenage baby drag she was known for her unique style. As she's grown older it's become more eccentric. One of the reasons the three of us get on so well is that The Big W and I are both far too polite to criticise. It would be a waste of time. Part of Lauren's charm is her infuriating ability to ignore the rest of the world.

What we didn't predict was Craig, Lauren's uncomfortable escort. He looks exactly like what he is, a teenage rugby league player, clean-cut, scrubbed and fitted into a rented tux for an awards night. Craig, not unexpectedly, has nothing to say.

We finish the first bottle of champagne as we glide over the Glebe Island Bridge to the soulful sounds of Barry White and the Love Unlimited Orchestra. The Big W has terrible taste in music but since she's paying for the limo, the soundtrack is hers. It doesn't matter. We're excited and not just because we all pilled and powdered before leaving home. When viewed through a limo's tinted windows, the world is wonderful. The harbour looks like that Brett Whiteley painting, all deep blue, fringed with rhinestone lights.

'You know,' I gush, squeezing The Big W's knee, 'if Sydney was a person, it'd be a drag queen. This is heaven.'

'Glamour is its own reward,' she replies. 'I knew you'd love it.'

The warm leatherette and chemicals are also working for Craig. He becomes increasingly animated. He can't keep his fingertips off Lauren and seems fascinated by the feel of her skin, her synthetic hair and the mixed media of her frock. She doesn't seem to mind, indeed looks quite contented. It's rare Lauren finds trade willing to dance attendance beyond the boudoir. I'm pleased for her, maybe even a little jealous. Craig is perfect.

'One day I'd like to get laid on the back seat of a limo,' I announce wistfully. 'I reckon it'd be just brilliant.'

'Especially if you fancied him,' purrs Lauren.

'Not some fat old businessman,' Craig says and giggles. 'That wouldn't be romantic.'

'They'd have to be sexy,' says Lauren. 'Not just filthy rich.'

'I hate that,' says Craig and continues stroking her neck. 'I hate those old guys who buy you a drink then sleaze all over you. They're gross.'

'And what will you do when you're old?' asks The Big W.

'Use credit cards,' Craig replies and picks up the mobile phone. 'Can I call some friends?'

'Go for it.'

But he can't remember anyone's number.

The champagne runs out just as we turn into Oxford Street.

'This is it kiddies. My next big surprise for you. We're on,' says The Big W. 'Frederico's making a movie. About me. He's going to be filming my arrival. Lauren and Craig first, then Grace and me. Get out slowly, pause, acknowledge the

167

camera and crowd, a smile and a brief wave should suffice, nothing sluttish Lauren, then motor forward to the doorway. Like the royal family do.'

In no time at all we've crossed Crown Street. Lauren and Craig look slightly bewildered. The Big W checks her face in her purse mirror and I check my fly is done up. We slow down to the sight of nothing but a line of parked cars in front of the unlit entrance to the venue.

'The bitch promised. He said I'd be in it,' shrieks The Big W. 'No one move. Wait right here.'

We double-park, causing a bank-up of traffic and much honking of horns while she dashes into the building. A long minute later she's back with the news that he's having trouble with his spotlight leads and wants us to drive up to the nearby bus stop in about fifteen minutes.

And so begins our slow cruise around the city and inner eastern suburbs. The Big W lowers her window and tells the driver to take it slow. She regally waves to the pedestrians. As we pass the cinema complexes, people wave back. Somewhat encouraged, she continues waving as we take the back route to Flinders Street and down to Taylor Square. In Darlinghurst the masses stop, face the road and cheer. She insists on a lap of the block so we can drive by these enthusiastic people once again.

'I feel immortal tonight,' she announces. 'I'm so glad you're all here to witness it.'

We stop at a bottle shop for more champagne. Craig shouts something common to a couple of his mates working The Wall and is told to behave himself or he'll be out walking with them.

Coming down William Street, we get stuck in traffic. Two large drags in full stage costume totter on impossibly high stilettos towards the limo, waving their arms in the air and shouting, 'Please, Big Madge. Please.'

'We're late and she's twisted her ankle,' pleads the taller of the two, a sylph-like figure in a leather mini and vest topped with a towering beehive.

'Please, darl, I don't think I can walk it,' puffs her partner, a much dumpier character, all feathers and sequins with a Spanish headdress. She leans on the side of the limo, trying to catch her breath.

'It's Marge and Homer Simpson,' says Lauren unkindly.

They ignore her and continue begging The Big W to let them join us.

'Please. Please.'

I can't help smiling. The short one looks just like the ugly Spanish princess in a fairytale I was read as a kid.

'Hail a taxi,' suggests Craig.

'Hire a forklift,' suggests Lauren.

'Please. Look, she's crippled. Completely challenged. Show some mercy.'

'Please Big Madge. Please . . .' begs the ugly Infanta.

The Big W says nothing.

'We don't want to miss seeing you get that award.'

The Big W beams and opens the door.

The limo seems extremely overcrowded. The driver is running out of patience. It's finally dawned on him that The Big W would be happy to spend all night aimlessly cruising the streets of Sydney waving at mug punters. He drives straight to Oxford Street.

Our second coming looks like being more interesting than the first. This time there's a panic in the limo. Everyone, except for Craig and I, is trying to make last minute adjustments to their outfits. Handbag mirrors are passed around and the air is filled with sickly hairspray.

'There goes the ozone layer,' I comment.

'I'd like to be green,' says The Big W, 'but it doesn't match anything in my wardrobe.'

'I worry about the ozone layer,' says Craig.

'And so you should,' says the Infanta, pushing him aside in an attempt to put her headdress back on.

'Can't you fix that hideous thing when you get out?' says Lauren, dragging Craig back next to her.

'No. Not if I'm being filmed . . . Anyway, as I was saying, boys, like this little stunner here, who spends all day lying by the pool, well *they* should worry about the ozone layer. But *we* are creatures of the night. You ever heard of a showgirl with skin cancers?'

'Some creature of the night,' says her partner, forcing me up against the door as she straightens her long legs to adjust her stockings. '*She* works in the food hall at David Jones. Like I always say, what a friend we have in cheeses.' She pauses, waiting for a laugh that doesn't eventuate.

'Glamour glamour, hit it with a hammer,' says her fuller-figured friend. 'And look who's talking. By day this one sits in an insurance office in a three-piece men's suit.'

'But *this* creature of the night can't even get herself transferred upstairs to Cosmetics. *She's* stuck behind a cheese counter forever. And that's why *her* skin's so white.'

'And why *her* arse is so wide,' mimics Lauren, pushing it out of her face.

We stop with a jolt. Before the driver can get to it, someone opens the door and, being nearest, Craig and I stumble out with little dignity. I can't see a thing. Someone is shouting at me to move out of shot and someone is holding a spotlight right in my face. I cross the pavement with my head down wondering how Princess Margaret manages to smile and wave in such circumstances. No wonder she took to drink.

When I turn I see a tall skinny man precariously perched on the curved roof of the bus shelter, holding a large video camera. He's shouting at a Lycra-clad lad who is now poking the spotlight into the face of each emerging diva.

Frederico, the man on the roof, is not happy. He makes all the glamour stars get back into the limo. The boy with the light is told to stay 'out of shot', back against the building wall. Craig is told that when he hears the word 'action', he is to walk towards the limo, open the door and bow slightly as each big wig gets out.

It sounds simple, but it isn't. It takes three attempts just to get the lighting lad positioned correctly. Even then Frederico's unimpressed, but says it will have to do. Apparently quality requires script development funding, which, like a decent spot or flood, is something this doco doesn't have.

By the fifth (and final) attempt, there's a large crowd spilling out onto the road, attracted like moths to the light. They are clapping and cheering like mad, jockeying to be in frame behind the action. Watching from the sidelines, it occurs to me that my four seconds of fame have been snatched away at the last moment and I wonder why I feel slightly miffed.

The venue is packed. We stand at the edge of a teeming sea of spectacularly over-dressed patrons who all seem to be industriously mingling, working the room at a furious pace. I take a deep breath, trying to quell a wave of claustrophobia. The main dance area is filled with long tables and as many chairs as possible. The Big W has booked seats right at the front (for easy access to the stage).

'Once we're down there, there's no escape, short of dancing along the tabletops,' she explains.

'Given the price of drinks here, that's unlikely,' says Lauren.

'Anyway,' continues The Big W, 'I suggest G&Ts then a quick pee before the squeeze to the "A" table.'

'You nervous?' I ask.

'Of course not. Just get me a double gin.'

It's easier said than done. The area facing the main bar is crowded beyond endurance. Halfway there, I can't breathe and decide to give up and retreat to the stairs to the mezzanine floor.

I bump into Brian attempting to do the same thing. His bar skills must be better than mine, he's carrying a drink. Or maybe someone bought it for him, he's that kind of guy. We end up crushed against the railing.

'So what have you been up to?' he shouts, hoping to be heard above the music.

'You know. Doin' the do . . .' I shout back.

'Where's Pointy Head?'

'In heaven. Died last year.'

'I'm sorry. I didn't know . . .'

He keeps shouting and I stop concentrating. My intention is to have a good night out and retelling stories about the last days of Mr Pointy Head aren't on the agenda. It takes forever for his lips to stop moving. He ends with some question about what exactly happened.

'He got sicker. He died. We had a funeral. It's a shame he's not here. He'd love all this.' I point to the seething pond of glamour below us.

'That's partly why I came tonight. Kind of hoped I'd run into him. OK if I ring you during the week?'

'You've got my number.' I don't mean to sound bitchy but Pointy left behind a whole address book full of people who meant to see him and didn't over his last year or two. It's quite chic in some het circles to have known at least one person who's died of AIDS. Like wearing a red ribbon, it proves you are a deeply liberal, caring person and means nothing.

'I lost touch with all of you. We moved around so much.'

It is possible he simply lost track of us. I can feel myself softening. 'Ring me during the week. Now isn't the time.'

'OK.' He puts an arm around me, squeezes my shoulder and leans against me. I don't mind at all. Sometimes it's easier when you don't use words.

I remember Pointy's nickname for him. The Fearless Fruit Fly. They recognised each other as soul brothers the first time they met. In 1986 Brian was an 18-year-old legitimate blond with a wardrobe of tight Levis and loose singlets. No one minded paying for his drinks, dinner and drugs in exchange for the privilege of having him around. Unlike Mr Point Head, he didn't cocktease or have brief affairs with his benefactors, but they did both share an innate expectation that the richest person should always pick up the tab. Back then, fruit flies like Brian were rare. Straight boys were either cheap prostitutes or bashers, easily identified by their (similar) dress sense. These days, fruit flies are endemic, each and every one a card-carrying member of Mardi Gras.

Frederico's camera and single spotlight are slowly panning from one side to the other of the crowd below us. As they move there's a slow motion frenzy of discreet violence as fabulously costumed people elbow each other out of the way in order to remain in the limelight.

'Great turnout,' Brian says. 'That's the thing about the gay scene. The whole community bit. You guys really care. I think that's important.'

I nod. It looks like a snake pit to me. I think it's time I had a long holiday.

'You here with someone?' I shout.

'No. Solo. What about you? Who's your date?'

'The Big W. You remember her. Big Madge. She used to compere shows here. Now she does homecare.' He nods. 'She's getting an award tonight. I'm her escort. I got to ride here in her stretch limo.'

'Sounds great.'

'Have you ever had sex in a limo?'

He hesitates before answering, 'No. Why?'

'Just wondering. I think I'd like it, that's all.'

I spot the Big W waving in the crowd. She signs that it's time to get to our table. I sign back, asking if it's OK to bring Brian. She nods, gives me the thumbs up then joins her hands as if in prayer and mimes thank you to the mirror ball above her. Like Noah, The Big W prefers everyone to be partnered.

The squeeze to the front isn't easy for those who chose a fuller costume. The Big W was right; once seated, it's impossible to move. We aren't at the "A" table, but are close enough to check out who did get there.

'What's the fascination with suits?' I ask. 'I don't think I've ever fancied a man for his suit.'

'It's what it stands for,' says the dyke journo sitting opposite. 'Money power, influence. It's a signifier.'

'We're born naked, the rest is drag,' quotes Lauren.

'Exactly,' says the journo.

'But I don't find them erotic,' I explain.

'You're a child of the 1970s,' says The Big W, 'not the 1990s. Modern gay boys date suits. It's what they do till they find one with a suitable apartment. Then they live together. Opposites attract. One has the suit and the harbour view, the other has the looks, and of course, the place to himself during the day.'

The conversation quickly descends into lurid gossip about the private lives of several of the more ostentatious junior fliers. The show, when it finally starts, is almost an anti-climax.

I'm not a great fan of drag performance. As an art-form, it has limitations which are often obvious by the third or fourth torch song in a row. I do, however, enjoy the dialogue. There's the rapid-fire exchange between on-stage entertainers, second-rate Oscar Wilde banter always delivered with a stylised bitchiness that's heard nowhere else these days—'Stop applauding her, she'll think she's attractive,' and, 'Who did your hair, love, Pet World?'

Plus I'm fascinated by the verbal exchanges between the entertainer and the audience. The public is mere fodder, passive viewers enjoying first the terror of possible selection for humiliation, then the excitement of watching someone else being eaten alive. I don't fully understand why it works so well. The Big W says that subduing a drunken crowd and having them eat out of your hand is a bigger rush than any drug.

Tonight, however, audience participation is strictly limited. In between the musical numbers are presentations: Best Show, New Diva, Entertainer of the Year, Best Show Cast and so on. It's self-indulgent, which bothers no one. Indeed the splendour of the occasion doesn't intimidate a single celebrity who graces the stage. When it comes to drag, there are no under-achievers. For many the excitement simply enhances that moment when the chemistry works, it really is the Dorothy Chandler Pavilion, and they get to make the ultimate thank-you speech.

Finally it's time for the Oustanding Achievement award. The presenter, a prominent lesbian community personality, in a full-length gold lamé evening gown, strides to the microphone, slightly surprised (as always) at the standing ovation.

'She borrowed that from Dot,' says the feisty dyke journo.

'They must have taken it up two feet,' says Lauren, licking a piece of hessian that has fallen off her costume. 'And anyway, who did your wardrobe, darl?' She makes several unsuccessful attempts to get the hessian to stick back on.

The journo, generally noted for a low-key approach to matters sartorial (faded ACT-UP T-shirts and flares), tonight is Diana Rigged in full Mrs Emma Peel drag. 'Nothing wrong with a bit of cross-cultural fertilisation. Mind you, it might be coalitionist, but it's not at all comfortable,' she grumbles.

'Glamour isn't meant to be,' says Lauren, stuffing the fallen appliqué into her clutch bag.

The Big W is busy. She finishes her drink, opens her purse, checks her lippie in the tiny coke mirror, puts the mirror and lipstick back, pauses, then puts her cigarettes and lighter in as well.

'Can't trust anyone these days,' she mutters.

She snaps the purse shut and hands it to me.

'Mind this.'

On stage they're still talking about past winners. The Big W downs my drink and pushes back her chair. The envelope opening appears to be happening in slow-motion.

And the winner isn't The Big W. It's a former soap star who has appeared at numerous AIDS fundraisers over the past few years. She seems lost for words, then genuinely moved as she accepts the laser-cut Marilyn statuette for her volunteer work.

'Over these last ten years of pain, grief and togetherness, I'm just glad to be friends with some of the bravest people I know.'

Brian squeezes my left hand. I am squeezing The Big W's left hand.

'It's OK, darl,' she whispers and grabs her bag back.

'Oh well,' says Lauren. 'That's that. Still, there's always the Mardi Gras Hall of Fame. You should start lobbying tonight. Everyone's here.'

The Big W's face is an impassive mask.

The house lights dim as the next number starts. It's a real crowd pleaser. Two dykes, in shimmering red outfits, go to town on 'Just Two Little Girls From Little Rock'. Their pure 1950s vamping segues perfectly into 'Diamonds Are A Girl's Best Friend' and the one in the blond wig, backed by a multi-gendered chorus line, all in impeccable top and tails, brings the audience to their feet, shouting for more.

The Entertainer of the Year award comes as another surprise. The young winner, seated miles from the front, bursts into tears as the spotlights single her out. As she passes our table I can see that the tears are real. Someone offers her a box of tissues. At the foot of the steps to the stage she blows her nose loudly, tucks the tissue into her bodice and ascends to face her apotheosis.

The Big W proudly announces, 'I taught her everything she knows.'

'It must have been a short lesson,' replies Lauren. 'Everyone says she's braindead.'

'She's great,' says Craig. 'I've seen every new show she's done since I moved to Sydney last year. Everyone I know voted for her. She deserves to win.'

'He's right,' says The Big W. 'It's about popularity. Not IQ. She's worked hard. She deserves the gong.'

'I'm over it,' declares Lauren.

'What else is there!' The Big W retorts coldly.

I wish I'd drunk less in the limo. Lauren has a terrible habit of turning vile when really pissed. Handled the right way, she snaps out of it, but I'm now not capable of such delicate diplomacy. Nor, I'm sure, is The Big W, whose current mood, under the tits'n'teeth facade, is anyone's guess. I catch Craig's eye and glance at Lauren. Craig nods back at me and begins stroking her neck.

The show ends with at least eight performers on stage in full costume doing *The Wizard of Oz* to perfection. Characterised by a generous excess of colour and movement, this grand finale is stolen by one of the more deconstructed divas in a post-modern interpretation of the Wicked Witch of the West. This up-staging, the journo assures us, is an achievement that will be called performance art by her paper's theatre reviewer.

'That's what he calls anything drag that isn't a torch song,' she explains.

'There's nothing wrong with a good torch song,' says The Big W. 'In my day . . .'

'In your day, darling, we were in Vietnam and the troops needed a morale booster,' says Lauren. Craig is now biting his way up her left arm in a manner very reminiscent of Gomez Addams.

'It all went downhill after punk,' replies The Big W. 'Nina Hagen and Laurie Anderson are no match for a good Shirley Bassey number.'

'People still talk about my Laurie Anderson at Mardi '87,' Lauren retorts. Craig is biting her neck and appears to have at least one hand up her skirt.

'Definitely performance art,' says the journo, raising her eyebrows. 'In some venues you can't avoid it.'

'So what?' shouts Lauren. '*It* was fabulous. *I* was fabulous. That's all that matters.'

Craig pauses, lifting his head to quietly ask, 'Who is Laurie Anderson?'

The house lights finally come up and our end of the table is empty. The journo is interviewing the ex-soapie star. Craig is eating Lauren's mouth. And Brian is at the "A" table, filling a champagne glass while chatting to a prominent AIDS bureaucrat.

'Fickle,' I say. 'All the world's fickle.'

'Don't take it so seriously, darl,' says The Big W. 'Lighten up. All the world's a stage. You just motor left, motor right and pray you remember the lyrics.'

'Stop bullshitting. Everyone said the gong was as good as in your clutch-bag. You're allowed to have the bitter and twisteds.'

'I'm not bitter,' she snaps bitterly, then laughs and softens. 'A bit twisted maybe, but I'll survive. Others have survived worse.'

'We'll nominate you for an Order of Australia. Billie Jean got one. For community service during the crisis. You can be the first tranny with one.'

'It's been ten years last January since Mike died. It's not a crisis. It's a lifestyle. When they find a cure, I'll have to find another day job. Can't imagine myself in business-drag selling insurance. Or cheeses. I guess I've been lucky really. For the past decade I haven't had to hide who I am.'

'You could open a tranny training school. Classes in tuck and tape, deportment and fashion sense. God knows, it's needed.'

'No way. They take no notice of their elders and betters. Look at Lauren.'

Lauren is moving back and forth on Craig's lap oblivious to the fact that more pieces of leather and black hessian are peeling off. It's unclear exactly what is going on under the disintegrating layers.

'I taught *her* everything she knows, too,' continues The Big W. 'And look at it. An outfit held together by Superglue. And footwear one generally associates with the severely physically challenged . . . I don't know what that boy child sees in her.'

'Whatever it is, thankfully it's hidden. Otherwise they'll get thrown out. I don't think she's miming.'

Outside there's a cold wind blowing up Oxford Street and it's raining heavily. Small groups detach themselves from the huddled mass under the awning and dash for cabs or on to the next venue. The Big W and I watch the new Entertainer of the Year descend the stairs, surrounded by a large entourage of adoring fans. They disappear up the hill under a cluster of black umbrellas.

'Share a taxi?' The Big W asks.

'OK. My shout. Don't you want to go for coffee or a quiet drink first?'

'Nup. As it is I'll have a stinker of a hangover. I'm picking Stephen up at ten for his clinic appointment. May as well get a few hours sleep in.'

We glide back over the Glebe Island Bridge in silence.

'Thanks for tonight,' I finally say as the taxi turns into her street. 'You were right. I should get out more often. Maybe even find myself a decent boyfriend. Tonight was brilliant. Especially the limo. The stuff dreams are made of . . . Have you ever been laid on the back seat of a limo?'

'Once. It was years ago. He was a top billing American entertainer, out here on tour. We did all the big nightclubs in those days. Chequers. The RSLs. The Silver Spade. We were his support act. Anyway, he was some celebrity or other. Hung like a bull but otherwise totally forgettable. As I recall I ended up on the limo floor. It was . . . very bumpy . . . Just here driver.'

I walk around the taxi and open her door.

'I still fancy the idea.'

'Then do it! It's easy. Pick up a boy. Ring the hire car company. Presto. A dream come true.'

She kisses me goodnight and I get back into the taxi.

'Did you have a speech prepared?' I ask.

'Of course. I've had my acceptance speech rehearsed since I was ten.'

ELEGY

JOHN A. SCOTT

Now Dolma writes to tell me A——
has become pregnant by an animal.
It is impossible. But I also know that
it will come to pass. This judgment.

Carl Brouwer
Letters, November 1983

1

Quartier on *quartier*, winter keeps a cemetery prospect: stone after stone; cream,
grey; unsoftened by foliage. Trees exasperated. Trees reduced to several up-ended
things. Bird's feet. Whisk-brooms of trees.

A cloudmass hurtles grey and grey-
black above the grey and grey-cream. It
passes by the windows of the studio as if
a curtain has been drawn.

Rue Campagne Première.

Fine scratches of rain appear against
the glass. Before the glass, the white of
potted cyclamen.

'Do you know what a city is?' she asks—as she had asked on that December afternoon, a month before.

She draws upon the cigarette, then lets the smoke roll upwards from her mouth. It moves about her hair; a soft blue scarf. It enlivens her.

'A city is a tension in breadth and a tension in height. Nothing else.'

*

'As a child—it would have been just before the war—I can recall looking out over Montparnasse. There had been heavy rains; enough to fill the *Cimetière du Sud*.' Her voice came from behind. 'From the window you could see the private sepulchres that line the cemetery avenues. I can remember watching young men push their way out between the iron-lacework doors, dressed in bathing costumes. Or perhaps it was a dream.'

I watched her slow descent: the gloss of dress, a shift; the leaving of an after-image, figure upon figure, as if the perfume had embalmed her absences. Blue-mauve. Beaded chiffon rouched against the hip.

I watched the slow elaboration of her movement; a self in its procession; more majestic, how it is performed in music halls:

Les petites filles de Camaret
Are virgins every one, they say . . .

She was in her seventies. A face of clay
on which she had fashioned for herself a
scarlet mouth. And cheeks of scarlet. Her
hair was built like spun toffee; though
drained of colour to a sunless grass.

'I'd sing and I'd dance for them; with
my scarf—which I slid across my shoulders
as if to say, "It's not so bad, what I'm
singing here." And they would pass the
bowler hat!

'I had a good ear, but a bad memory.
I cannot see how these women could sing
as easily as they urinate! *Monsieur*?'

I held the proffered hand a moment,
before bringing it to my lips. I observed
a previous courtesy: the cancers gently
kissing at her skin.

Dolma.

We sat, much as we sit today; a blade of
pale sun, riddled with lace, giving flesh to
air, blue with tobacco.

She too had noticed it.

'At *The Jockey* you would have to go
for air, from time to time . . . out onto
the Boulevard . . .'

She had pulled her hem, extravagantly
enough, above the knees—which had
been rouged for the occasion.

'. . . and then another plunge into the
smoke of endless countries. Copeland with

his cowboy songs, or Hiler. And if Hiler didn't play, we would grab the silverware and clank three spoons together . . .

'You bring me *other* dreams,' she said, and placed her cigarette upon the tray.

'Recently, I read the cards. She had returned—hung from the sky, her dresses billowing. And there were journeys . . . Other dreams. More brutal dreams, I fear.'

She must have recognised it from where she sat: his letter; scrawled out upon its single sheet; every space—as if the whiteness of a page had terrified him—infested with confession.

A bleak smile moved her face—the prowling sun that strengthens for one moment to find endless detail in a bald monotony of plane—and then everything subsided to the grey-cream of this earlier December afternoon.

'He was, I make no secret of it, one of my favourites. He had that exquisite lunacy of the men I saw about me in my childhood. Where these days do you find such risk? Such jokes? Such capacity for ruination?'

She brought the paper slowly to her face; so close to make me fear, a moment, she might eat it.

I sought her yellowing, clouded eyes. And were these weathers (I considered), clouded, yellowed—their cataract across the city—consequent upon her failing sight; come, like a dream, to flood this emptiness with view? I watched her turn the letter back and forth. She paused.

'This judgment,' she repeated, reaching for the cigarette. 'And you still wish—and after all that has occurred—to seek her through the child? And even *there*? You wish to journey to this other place?

She sat silently a moment; head averted from the smoke, turned slightly to the left and upwards, as if in expectation of another voice.

'You are aware of the precise nature of the child?'

I had imagined (not what she was soon to say) something possibly short-lived. And cloven. Bristling underneath the smothering-cloth. And not the words that she would use.

'I have heard,' she said, 'that it is something of a god.'

'I have had innumerable lovers—but then I had the fortune to be born into the world of lovers! How they fall in love, these artists and their models; all the endless *coups de foudre*! But (it is a cliché) I have seldom *loved*.

'Modi, of course, I loved. He was the most handsome man in Montparnasse! And I was barely twelve. I would rouge my lips and cheeks with petals from an artificial geranium and sit waiting for a glimpse of him at *La Rotonde*.

'Modi, yes. And Camini.'

The lamp flickered, as if the name had snatched, a second, electricity from the room.

'I started bleeding on the first day that I saw him. This was significant, yes? I felt that he had somehow brought it on, this violent *menarche*.

'He had been a painter then for many years. After the war there were no more construction sites: no singers there, no stalls, no prostitutes; no carvers to give limestone to the artists! Now his studio floor was covered with a carpet of coal, charcoal and matches.

'I modelled for him. My hair was badly developed in a certain place and I had to make myself up with black crayon.

'I would stand beside the window, drenched in winter light and I would stare, as he had asked me, down, away, across the makeshift corrugated roofing. My view would always end within a courtyard: dark; held in deep perpetual shadow. The walls were cracked with stains where ivy had been torn down from the bricks, I can recall the blackness. And a red scarf, like a wound against his throat.'

'Camini was the first I knew who sought this other place.

' "Do you know what a city is?" he said, the night of his departure. "A city is a tension in breadth and a tension in height. Nothing else.

"Every individual tries by whatever means: their legs, the train, a trolley, or explosives—that transportation of the future—to find the meeting point of these two tensions."

'It haunted him. He was in love with its extremity. *Un coup de foundre*!

'Then, after months of silence, I received a letter.

'It was brought to me, much as you have brought this other correspondence.

'A single white page; white, white; crossed through with two diagonal lines— an "X"—as if everything should be deleted.'

She rose from the divan and stood before me. Her body seemed quite suddenly to have gathered all its sparsity of fat to one small pouch, low on her abdomen; her form mis-shapen, it appeared, through the very act of telling.

'I shall bring the letter,' she announced. 'It is the only map of this place that I have ever seen.'

I watched her slow ascent towards the mezzanine.

The beginnings of a distant conversation came to me—at first, I thought, from an adjoining studio.

I heard the now-familiar emphases of Dolma's voice, insistent:

'Aldo, all the young men, all so recently enthralled!'

And then a deeper voice, more thickly accented—effeminate (I add with some amusement)—came in reply . . .

I had moved again towards the windows, their space reduced to tapestry by the decaying light. I had traced the wall (papered in a fading leaf—a spill of foliage shattered from a fallen stem), the lower edge angled by the skirting board; and, following the stairs, in that irregular pentagon of light created by the door, half-opened, to an upstairs room, I had seen Dolma, much a mannequin, yet answering herself in that impersonated voice: '. . . For all his different history, he is not so unlike Pogliani? No?'

2

Two straight connecting wires depict a city.

Camini (as I.K. Bonset)
Towards a Constructive Poetry, 1923

Air drenched with the metallic taste of electricity, building and releasing in explosive clicks. A tongue snapped from the palate.

The *guardien*'s cigarette-end drops

diagonally—a sudden click—its path veers back; the ash striking at the floor: a ricochet of powder zig-zagging on the stone like an escaping lizard.

Pulsing cones of loudspeakers crackle their repeated anthem to the re-touched face of General Pesce—liberator, saint— his cheeks resplendent in their twenties rouge.

Quartier des Echafauds. Every body-chime congested with a shimmering of wings. A swaying, raucous black.

Shriek of mandrakes. Streets littered with their roots. Restless, still-tumescent tubers bursting underfoot; the surface of their skin like magnified hair.

Along the avenues, the Titans, massive, perfectly proportioned, clamber from the billboards; their clothing riddled with decay; their skins, once tanned and oiled, grown pale and torn.

They fall strengthlessly upon the street. Their faces fold upon themselves.

The insects gather.

Undeniably, towards the second hour of dusk (How dusk? This resin soaking through the flapping rags of sky.) a machine, bizarre in the intricacy of its clockwork, approached from the horizon: the model of a solar system—a sun, flamboyant in its gesturing, surrounded by the eccentric orbits of some seven lesser bodies.

A voice, distorted by the snapping air, called out to me across the plain, as if we shared some common purpose.

'You are heading for the hospital? *L'hôpital de la Conception?* Too far!' he cried. 'A journey to the hospital at such an hour would be unthinkable.'

I watched him lurching out towards two of his assistants, ordering them to make a pile of their equipment.

'Can't you see my friend is very tired? You must carry him!' he trumpeted. 'Are you incapable of hearing? Leave the lights! Marcel, enough of this! My fellow traveller must be carried to the villa. *Allez! Allez!*'

Pogliani.

'I loathe the hospital. The wire.' He stopped. 'Most of all, I loathe the sound of wire, the movement back and forth. It is the rupturing of everything I know. Of civilisation. Of hope. Of desire.'

Then possibly his hand began to speak. Of course not. Just the bubbling of the hookah: smoke procuring its wraith passage through the staining water.

'He has become a skeleton. His right arm is completely useless and most of the left. They give him shocks with some electric apparatus: the hand twitches—then it might as well be *cabillaud*. Last time his back was completely flayed from the bed.

'Nonetheless, he gives permission for the filming. I tell him I adore his poetry. I tell him that the BBC has shown an interest.

'He talks, but he is evasive; everything is metaphor. I have had cartons of his prattle transcribed.'

Pogliani sat bolt upright in his chair. 'And I have searched it thoroughly for hidden meanings!'

I stared at the Italian's forearms: a baroque profusion. A brooding cashmere in the oil-light of the study. The colour of his hair. The colour of burnt almond, shot through with the black-red of drying blood.

It was his surfaces that seemed to crave description: the flocculence of arms; the stubble; and the duskiness of skin.

And yes, a detail: a crescent scar upon the cheek—and held between the tips, a mole. I contemplated it with a certain mariner's affection. And that he was dressed in a safari suit; as if he were a hunter.

'So Dolma sends you here,' he smiled. 'You know she was Camini's lover in the twenties—during his so-called "abstract" period, yes? And that she came with him, to *Xei*, as it was called in those days . . . Have you read the history of this place?'

He leaned forward, conspiratorially. 'It was for many years the furtherest city of the Roman Empire . . . He arrived, December 1923, and he began to film.

'You know too well what the city chose to show him.'

Pogliani stared at me, as if I should have understood the subject of his speech.

'It frightened him. He assembled everything into the documentary as though it were his last confession. And then silence.'

He paused, perhaps providing me with space in which to add my own confession. I listened to the persistent bubbling of the hashish as if we might have passed below the surfaces of air and were conversing underwater. Yes. This would have helped explain the slowness of our movements; the impediments to the passage of words; the sound of the chair against the wooden floor reaching me too late, as if the noise had been retained, perhaps distracted, by some unseen listener and released a moment later—the original sounds already having started to decompose. I listened to the rotting of his voice.

'It was the documentary that led me to the arms of Dolma.

'I can recall each moment of that languid afternoon in Paradise.

'We sit beside the windows of her studio. Her knees are rouged for me. She is showing me a nude she modelled for

Massoni. A child of fourteen—but I notice how the brushstrokes have a sense of purpose. I turn, to see the dress fall first from one shoulder, then the other.

' "I find the brassière to be a troublesome and modern bondage," she announces. And she smears the last of mauve sateen across her ribs into a gathering below the waist. I hardly need remind you that she is a person in her seventies. The breasts belong upon a goat!

'However, I decide that I shall ginger the occasion. I croon her name as if I were her lover from the twenties. I lift her sparrow body in my arms and drape her on the counterpane. I spread her hair—you know, of course, the quite insufferable nature of her hair—I *place* what hair I can across the pillows. I anticipate the marbling of the lower fleshes. I say, "Ah, how age performs its alchemy: this flesh to precious stone!"

'And my beloved Dolma slowly rolls onto her belly. Using both her hands pressed tightly to her thighs, she slides the chiffon skirt above her buttocks. I can see the wrinkled genitalia hanging loosely in between her legs like some malignant afterbirth!'

He stopped. He burst into ferocious laughter: 'She is a man!'

'Of course, I had no choice. You can imagine it was sickening. For weeks afterwards

I found it quite impossible to defaecate without the memory returning.'

I watched his hand fall open: an old man's mouth; a drool of sweat between his curving finger and the thumb.

'It was a rather bald exchange: my knowledge of the film for what she knew about the angel.

'But I have kept you in suspense too long. No doubt you must be anxious to observe this footage for yourself.'

'I have in my possession the second-last reel—you can imagine at what cost— nonetheless, the crucial evidence is here.'

Pogliani threaded the projector.

'At Lecce, I have all Camini's earlier work . . . the cubist animations.'

'And the paintings?'

Pogliani halted in his preparations.

'You must excuse me, but I have never heard of any painting. It is possible, of course; but Camini worked in film, as *I* do. If you know of the existence of a painting . . .'

I remarked that Dolma had implied a work, or possibly I had mis-heard; misunderstood her reference.

'Or possibly she keeps a little secret from me? We must discuss these rendezvous in further detail!'

And he turned the light.

The whirr began. The metal teeth lodged

and then discharged from the sprocket holes. The brittle nitrate film unwound its shifting mouldered chiaroscuro across the lamp.

We were in a stark and windowless enclosure; the ceiling typically vaulted, as if the walls had curved with the accumulation of these gravities.

A single wooden table. On its surface lay a figure; naked; the belly grossly distended; thrust by its own contents into the greater distortions of the room.

IL PARTO È LUNGO E DOLOROSO

Pogliani leant forward slightly, translating.

'The labour is long and full of pain.'

We had moved closer to the centre of the room. In the background, hazed by focus, two robed figures were preparing a solution in a shallow pottery saucer, their bodies swaying slightly: a drawn curtain disturbed by gathering wind. In the foreground . . .

A further title appeared.

'The moment is at hand!' cried Pogliani with such enthusiasm I was not sure if this was his own exclamation or whether he was merely offering the sense.

We had returned to the shaved flesh of the genitals; in such extreme close-up there was a momentary loss of detail: the vagina dark and puckering. Like a pink.

'Miracolo dei miracoli!'

I caught Pogliani's transfixed face, bathed in the reflections of projected light.

I looked back to see the child expelled in a caul: the pouch of membrane resting pupae-like between its bearer's legs.

I peered down on the smothered surface, detecting in the ravellings of flesh perhaps the legs, the torso of a child.

The head curved into view. The snout displayed its teeth. It bit against the membrane and the fluid broke, dissolving all the view into a streaming light.

I caught the creature, with the half-flap of its yet-unfeathered wings, lumbering to the frame's edge, where it disappeared into the rust of the emulsion.

The distortion of the woman's genitals had been immense, lending the appearance of a withered penis—not unlike how Dolma's sex had been described by Pogliani. Then suddenly the image flared to white; and there was nothing but the sharp and brittle slap of film-tail, thrashing from its spool against the projector.

The lights had been restored. Pogliani showed increasing agitation, as if he were full-bladdered with some additional detail.

'What was it, do you think, you followed here? What blacker star? What were your gifts?

'The answers are of little consequence,

my friend,' he gasped. 'Your search has been too late!'

He pulled me by my collar from the room.

The tangled threads that were our shadow, hooped the surface of a narrow passage-way.

A seepage, oil-slow, had collected underfoot. I watched the splash of Pogliani's boots—liquid peeling off the surface like a membrane from raw liver.

'Your eyes will soon become accustomed to the light,' he said. 'Look there!' And faced me at the darkness.

'Do you think that Pogliani has been burdened with his predecessor's fear? Another little Aldo, quivering at his editing machine?

'I have a trophy of the voyage, and have brought damnation down upon my head for what I have achieved.

'Can you see it?'

My eyes drew out appearances from shadow. Convinced themselves of fore-ground, background; of the fact amongst this shamble of improbability.

There was a cage.

'But what is there inside the cage?'

Air warmed by a faecal stench. A memory of circus.

He thrust the lamp towards the space

ahead of us, ejaculating into childish laughter.

'Look! There is an angel!'

'At first the constant battering of wings against the bars caused frightful, I fear permanent, damage. I doubt for instance now, that it could fly.

'Consequently, there were certain measures forced upon me . . .'

Behind the bars I momentarily caught the nightmare vision of a jackal god, its wings outstretched in pale embracement. Then other details came to me.

The creature was restrained within a wooden frame, the hind legs barely reaching to the floor and flicking upwards in involuntary spasms.

A black wig had been fitted to its head. The wings were mere theatrical effect: a gathered sheeting draped across the shoulders and outstretched on wooden poles.

In one particular, Pogliani had been right: it could not fly. I watched as the director knelt before the suffering creature.

'Sing,' he gently crooned. 'My angel, sing to me.'

I slept perhaps a single hour. An hour pervaded by a vivid and recurrent dream in which Pogliani's angel, now grown

whole, broke free of its restraining brace:
the sheets become a feathered flesh; the
wig, a mane. I watched its halfflapping,
shuddering passage—thrashing through
the liquids—back along the milky-pink-
ness of the corridors.

I saw Pogliani sit up in his bed and
vomit.

I saw the angel leap, half-flapping, to
the covers where it stood astride the
director, trampling the sheets, kicking up
its twiggish feet, as if engaged in some
outrageous Charleston.

I watched it tear out Pogliani's heart—
a scarlet, fibrous tuber—and carry it, half-
flapping in between its jaws, towards a set
of balances that hung above the bed-end.

I watched it spit the still-beating
object to the metal of the tray. I saw it
weighed against a feather. And I saw that
Pogliani's heart was heavier.

I fell awake; a squib-glimmer of light
pattering at the shutters, like a moth.

For a final time I retraced the passage
to the dog-cell (and what if I had found
the creature absent?) moving back along
the wave-form surface of the walls.

Behind the bars, the creature shuddered convulsively on its frame. And it was
such, that should I have asked, 'What do
you want?' it surely would have answered
this:

'I want to die.'

*

At the hospital, a group had gathered in the courtyard.

'*L'estropié*!' they cried towards the arches of the balcony. *Where is the amputee?*

The sky was gathering about them: darkly puckered and then slackening—a breathing; bulging down in loops of rippling cloud.

It was the mother-dress, full and billowing. It was the shroud.

It was another curtain ready to be drawn.

I waited the remainder of the day amongst the milling people, holding to the bars.

As evening drew the last of light to earth, the poet's sister made a brief appearance on the balcony.

Her lips had been disfigured; punctured through with wooden splinters as a token of her grief. As if she understood that speech could only now be undertaken at the cost of pain.

She spoke, the flaps of skin stretching up and back with each deliberate word.

'I talked with him, for some time, as you would have wished. I give you these, his final words, dictated to me thus, an hour before his death:

one tusk only
two tusks
three tusks
four tusks
two tusks.

*

The fiction that I brought condolences from Pogliani seemed of little interest to the *guardien*.

'*Les femmes soignent ces féroces infirmes retour des pays chauds*,' he smiled. 'You'll find her in the galleries. She has requested *les embaumers*.' He breathed forcefully through the nose. 'It is ridiculous, when there's so little left to be preserved! At least the stench will make her easier to find.'

He pushed a torch across the counter's ivory.

There was a single staircase cut from stone; a narrowing spiral, as if the workers had grown increasingly impatient with their task; these hundred steps that fed me deep beneath the hospital.

Crystals had begun to form within my joints: a gout induced, presumably, by breath.

The stairwell flattened to a single tunnel, curving out of view and downwards to the right. These were the now-familiar surfaces of the underground: the pink-white from the corridor at Pogliani's villa.

I advanced in loping strides, stooped by a ceiling gouged out to a height barely above five feet. My jacket pressed itself against my back—then billowed wilfully: a line of wet, half-flapping linen. A slow arc of torchlight swerved across the walls: the yellowed beam too weak against the airless gales of gravity.

And then, illuminated for a second, I glimpsed the letters forming 'RUE', obscenely carved into the stone-face.

(Here are rose-flanked pathways; here, the flower-named detention camps.)

These streaming gutters dignified as streets.

And soon the torch found other half-named passages—a 'QUINE', a 'RASPAI'—amputated from the body of this stolen city.

Now I chose the turning filled with dogs.

Now I chose the bellowed laughter.

And the stench.

*

I had made her bleed.

The wooden splinters tugged at her speech like an impatient child; delaying

every syllable, as if she were entranced;
every word a wound's re-opening; every
word a fresh annointing of the blackening
layers stepped down from her mouth.

I had become her priest.

'During the chaos of Pesce's revolution—
who knows,' she said, 'perhaps occasion-
ing it—a child was born . . . as some
would have it, an *unnatural child* . . . and
was delivered from this place . . .'

And did she mean this city? Or this
hospital? Or even from this room?

The poet's body, much as Pogliani had
described it, lay upon a wooden table in
the centre of the chamber.

The face was coated in hot resin. The
stiff wire used to slash the brain had been
removed.

One of the embalmers now began to
spoon the pulp out through the nostril
with a small cup-ended rod.

A stampede of odours.

A plague of mating air.

'I have heard my brother talk about an
earlier child,' she was continuing. 'I have
heard it perished shortly after birth, at the
hands of its attendants.'

The words became a momentary gar-
gling. Her hands reached to the splinters
and she pouted slightly, clearing the saliva
from her mouth.

'Both were born on heat, with jackal heads and wings . . .'

But I had seen this child. It was a mongrel strapped to a bondage brace. The wings were sheet.

Perhaps it was the eyes—how else could I have read that answer as a smile?

'So, you have visited the sideshow. I have heard of Pogliani's masterpiece. It is a mockery.'

Behind her, the robed figures of the embalmers burst into usual laughter. A joke about the genitals.

On the table end, wedged between the poet's thighs, a bag of fluid—body seepage—bulged out like some excessive scrotum.

'No,' she said, oblivious to their *raillerie*, 'the true child lives.'

She paused.

'It shall grow to be the Angel of Extermination.'

She stared at me as if to dare a contradiction.

'That was the vision of our brother's final poem.'

I glanced towards the half-legged body.

'You think this was some reverie of fever? The amputation was for him the perfect disordering of the senses.

'The years in exile were a necessary preparation; the love, the suffering, the madness; the consuming of the poison;

the charge through those unutterable, unnameable things . . . all to reach the unknown: *here*. "The time of the assassins" as he once described it.'

She paused again, re-bearded in her blood.

I watched the slashing of the poet's abdomen; the thrusting of hands into the cut; the gathering of the stomach and intestines.

'This was not hallucination. He was present at the birth you came to seek. But for him the act was merely confirmation. Our brother—the great criminal and *malade*, the great accursed!—understood there is no difference between the poem and barbarity.'

'Qebhsenuef!' bellowed the embalmer, the slippery ropes of flesh unravelling through his arms, 'Qebhsenuef! You son of a whore!'

The assistant brought a limestone jar.

'I was with him for those final hours. It began with disgust and it ended with a riot of perfumes. It began with *rustrerie* and it has ended with the angel.'

I listened to this talk of the apocalypse, garbled in the black-red boxer's mouth that gaped, opening and half-opened, ruined at her face.

'I doubt,' I said, 'that ours is such a time of myth.'

There was a brief hiatus. I watched her

stand. I watched as she drew the wooden splinters, one by one, slowly through her lips, placing them beside the oils, the adze, of the embalmers. I watched her move towards the bed.

Isabella bent towards her brother's broken mouth and kissed him. A lover's kiss. She straightened; turning to me; her lips now streaming with the fluids she had occasioned from his body. It was as if her face had given birth.

'*Monsieur*,' she said, the words now bilging from her mouth, 'we have faith in our poison. It has the same name as our kisses. It has the same name as this city.'

I closed the door upon her grief—that metaphysick of hysteria.

I moved, amongst the milling dogs, along the walls. The torchlight slashed against the streetsign of the gallery. I pressed my fingers deep within the wet slits of stone, tracing out the name.

It was familiar: as if the genitals of someone once beloved; someone known for many years, whom one had come eventually to loathe.

3

The wind had dried all but the largest drops of rain: each holding in its sphere a portion of the lightness and the darkness of the afternoon.

There is a sudden squall. The rain becomes smoke.

'It is the signature of the illiterate. It is perverse. It is illicit. It is the heart of the unknown, obliterating everything in its profusion.'

Dolma has unwound the soft blue scarf. The blue-mauve dress has slipped first from one shoulder, then the other.

'A poem is just like a city. The poet must make himself a new language with the alphabet: a language of great distances, of depth and height. The poet must construct his language with the ruins of the past . . .

'But enough of this, *ma chère fringille, mon frère.*'

She calls me, 'Aldo, you must kiss me, as you have come to do. And deeply.'

MY COCK LIVES IN HELL

TONY AYRES

For my fortieth birthday my wife, Serina, comes into the room with a cake the shape of a coffin. In the semi-darkness, Serina floats, her face and upper body illuminated by forty hand-painted black candles. What disturbs me is the detail—wood-grain walnut icing, a wreath of marzipan arum lilies, and a marzipan corpse with an uncanny resemblance to you know who, right down to the little round belly. A great deal of loving attention has gone into this creation.

The party is struck dumb. Johnno coughs and looks at his watch. Josie, who works with Serina at the bank, pours herself another Cinzano and Coke. Serina's sister, Elise, laughs, 'Come on, Bill, blow out the candles!'

Later Serina tries to explain it was a joke.

'No one laughed.'

'Elise did.'

'That stupid bitch wouldn't know if her twat was on fire.'

'Don't say that. I hate it when you use language.'

'Muff. Cunt. Twat. Hole.'

'Why do you deliberately upset me?'

'Who wheeled out the coffin, baby?'

Serina is sitting up in bed, smoking a cigarette. She has taken to wearing a frilly nightie, apricot with little white daisies stitched on. Spanish women think this is the ultimate in chic. I tell her it makes her look like an oven mitt.

'I told you. It was a joke!'

'Muff. Cunt. Twat. Fuck. Cunt. Cunt. Cunt.'

Soon after, Serina moves out. We met two years ago, queuing for the dole. I am still crazy for her. For a strict Catholic girl, she has some surprising assets. Like the way she sweats uncontrollably when she's excited. It's like fucking in Niagara Falls. And if you get her in the right mood, she'll dress up in sexy black lingerie and put a mirror beside the bed. Best of all is the grip on her sphincter muscles— you could crush a Coke can with that grip.

I fell into a funk. I didn't have a job. I was forty. The only bit of this city I liked was between my wife's legs. I hung around home, playing Russian roulette with the dog, wondering why things fuck up, and how I could meet another woman, when the phone rang.

'Hello? William? My name is Alain. I am a student of your sister, and she say if I am in Australia, I should ring . . .'

Fucking Kelly! She went off to be revolutionary in Paris in '68 and ended up marrying an Algerian Muslim, some kind of fundamentalist activist. She sent us photos of the wedding. She was head to toe in a brown sack. Needless to say, this did not go down a treat with Mum and Dad.

Dad—'How do we know it's her? It could be a fucking shop dummy.'

Mum—'Look at the toes, Dad. Ugly fat toes.'

Dad—'They could have cut her feet off and stuck them on a shop dummy.'

These day Kelly teaches English at a private college in Marseille. Every few years she sends a photo of her and a new milk-chocolate coloured baby with shiny, uncorrupted eyes. She never sends photos of the husband.

I ask Alain around for a beer, and he brings his backpack. He looks like he comes from a good home. He uses a sweet-smelling soap on his milky white skin. He has brown eyes and a chisel-jawed, unblemished face. His jeans are freshly pressed and he wears a lemon-yellow polo neck sweater. He's got nowhere to stay, so I let him nestle amidst the pizza boxes on the living room floor.

'I gotta warn you mate, I like to walk around in the raw.'

'Raw? You don't like to cook?'

'In the buff. The nuddie. Starkers . . .'

'Pardon?'

'Here, I'll show you.'

I think eventually the smell drives him out. There is a problem with the plumbing, we have no water and it is the middle of a stinking summer. After a couple of days, the place pongs of nonspecific body excretions. I take to showering at the bus station, where you can hire a cubicle for a couple of dollars. I invite Alain to join me. He politely declines.

The night before he leaves, I take Alain to Crystals. On Thursday nights they have the Ladies Only strip shows. I have heard that around 1 a.m. several hundred horny women pour on to the streets. I figure if you can't interest a woman under these circumstances, you may as well join a monastery.

According to my taxi driver friend, Johnno, most of the women go home in a herd, but every now and then, one of them split from the pack. One night he picked up a redhead who was so hot she went down on him before they got around the corner. She sucked on his candystick for an hour and Johnno, the bastard, left his meter running. I can't say whether this is true because Johnno is a pathological liar, but it has become part of Sydney taxi driver mythology, and the queue of taxis outside Crystals runs several blocks deep.

I don't drive a taxi anymore, so we hang around outside in the ball-breezing cold, hoping to pick up a few strays.

'Imagine all those women groping for your arse,' I say to Alain, staring at the closed door. We can hear muted shrieks of laughter and a flat disco bassline.

'Come out here, babes. You can have it for free!' I grab the outline of my dick for effect. I'm ready for anything—I'd been drinking since 4 p.m. A couple of the drivers toot their horns in encouragement.

'One day someone's gonna cut that thing off, Bill.'

'I'll just sew it back on, man!'

The French kid is hugging himself to stay warm, stomping his feet. Every now and then he grins. He's a handsome lad.

'Have you got a girl?'

'Pardon?'

'A girlfriend. Back in France.'

'Oh . . . no.' Smiling, shaking his head philosophically. For some reason he reminds me of a block of Nefutal cheese. 'Just a few casual friends.'

'What are they like? French women.'

'French women? Maybe they are more sophisticated. I don't know. Maybe the same.'

'More of the same. I don't need that.'

Just then the bouncer, a big Greek body-builder type, opens the doors. I feel an excitement building.

'Here they come.'

The women charge out. Women of all shapes and sizes. Young Greek girls with log-sized thighs in tarty short skirts and chandelier earrings. Blonde secretaries in shoulder pads and lipstick the colour of blood. Raisin-faced, white-haired old ladies creak along in knitted pink cardigans. They're laughing and clutching each other's arms—drunk, fearless, awesome.

I try to catch a few by the eye and say, 'Howdy,' in my best Oklahoma twang, but there are too many of them. It's like the first time I went roo shooting with my dad. 'Concentrate on one of them,' he said. 'Fix one in your sights and nail her.'

'Hey, did you enjoy the show?' I ask a muscly woman with a hooked nose who must work out five times a week.

'Show us your dick!' she screeches back, then laughs hysterically to her girlfriend.

'Come here and I'll show you something!' I call but they are well past.

'Where is your friend?' asks Alain. He is looking distressed. Four Jewish mamas have been trying to stick money down the front of his pants.

'What friend?'

'You say you come here to pick up a friend.'

This is the wrong time to explain.

'Just hang on.'

They're slipping past me, just like the roos used to. In all the times I went shooting, I never made a kill. Not a clean one. A few winged animals, splattering to the ground, wracked and twitching. Get one in your sights, my daddy used to say. But they refused to keep still, Dad.

'Australian women are very excitable,' Alain says, a little shocked.

'They're all whores.'

But there's one who maybe is not. She's one of the last out. The only woman by herself, wrapped up tight in a tatty fake-fur coat. She has a pretty, round Oriental face. Her head is bowed, as if not wanting to be recognised. I gather my wits.

'Hey sweetheart!'

She looks up, startled, then quickens her pace.

'Darling. You know it's dangerous walking the streets alone.' I am walking next to her. 'Where are you going?'

She turns her lotus blossom complexion in my direction.

'Please . . .'

Her face is powdered white, and at this distance I catch the faintest whiff of jasmine oil. Her black eyes are big. Open wide, vulnerable. I catch my breath. I stop. She faces down, hands clutching the coat to her throat, and walks quickly away.

Before she gets too far, I call out.

'What's your name?'

She turns for a parting glance but does not answer. Alain is next to me. He looks at me darkly.

'I do not think your friend needs to be picked up . . .'

The next day I return from the bus station to find Alain gone and a note on the kitchen table. 'Thank you for the good time, Bill. See you in Marseille.' It is accompanied by a small, gift-wrapped bottle of French deodorant. I feel a twinge of disappointment.

I hear a thump in the next room, and go to investigate, thinking that it's still the kid. Instead I find Serina sticking her shoes into a black-plastic garbage bag. Elise is piling clothes into another bag. When she sees me, Serina stiffens. Elise sets herself between us.

'Baby . . .' I whisper.

'We let ourselves in,' says Elise. 'Serina wanted to pick up some things.'

'Serina, can we talk?' I make a move towards my wife.

Elise raises her hand.

'Stay away from her.'

Serina looks like a little girl lost in a fairground. God, she is beautiful. I can't help it, I'm getting hard.

'I just want to talk, baby.'

I try to step around Elise.

'Don't touch her!'

Serina touches her face. The bruise is almost healed.

'Honey, you know I didn't mean it. I love you, Serina.'

This confuses her. She looks like she is going to cry.

'I can't Bill. I can't.' She grabs the bag and makes a run for it, past me, through the flat, out the door. Elise follows, spitting as she passes.

'If you touch her again, I'll kill you!'

Time stands still for me. Even after the door slams and I know she's gone again, I can't seem to move.

A couple of days later, I ring Nancy. She's an American I used to fuck. Before she got busted, Nancy owned a tanning parlour in San Diego. The week she got out of prison, she answered a personal ad from an Australian real estate broker in Brisbane. The marriage only lasted a few seconds, but she liked it here so she stayed. Now she works days at this fat ladies' boutique—she calls it the MM—the Massive Mammaries. Four nights a week she moonlights at a low-life dive called the Chauffeur's Club. Two things about Nancy: I never met anyone with a tan so deep, or who loved money so much.

'What do you want?'

'I was just wondering if you were lonely, honey. Maybe you wanted some company.'

'Jesus. After three years. You're lucky I can still remember who you are.'

'How could you forget me, babe? We had a good time, didn't we?'

'You know the thing I remember about you?'

I don't have time to answer.

'Your smell. I never met a man who smelled so much like dog shit. You wanna see me, you take a shower.'

I'm drinking scotch in Nancy's fancy white apartment over-looking the bay. She's sporting a brand new hair cut. Short at the sides and frost tipped, like Bridget Neilsen. Even in the middle of winter she's mission brown, wearing a sleeve-less white dress, loaded down with chunky silver jewellery. In her mid-forties, Nancy likes to dress young.

'I wouldn't recognise you,' she says, pouring herself another Black Label.

'I've changed.'

'You know, most men look younger without their beards.'

'You still got no heart, Nancy.'

She smiles a long reptilian smile and shows off her ten thousand dollar pearly white teeth.

'How are the girls?'

On the mantelpiece there's a photo of Nancy's identical twin daughters, Tanya and Marcie, who are television weather girls on some cable station in San Diego. 'Let's hear the weather in stereo.' Along with her personal solar-ium, they are Nancy's pride and joy.

'I got a card from them last week. They're up for a role as twin cheerleaders.' Nancy shrugs. 'Just as long as they don't do porn.'

She's got her long bare brown legs tucked under her on the sofa. I run my hand along them.

'God, you look good. How old are you?'

'Motherfucker.'

Later we do the deed. 'Fuck me. Fuck me.' She pulls me towards her, fingering herself into a fit.

'Just give me a second.' I wank my soft cock up and down in the rubber. 'Damn condoms.'

'Come on, come on, I'm burning. Give it to me.'

I flip her over onto her stomach, tugging up and down on the flaccid package.

'Hey, what are you doing? Don't stick it in my ass.'

'Just a bit. Go on, just the head.'

'No. Around here, that's it. Come on, what's wrong?'

'It's the damned condom. It's like a rubber glove.'

'Jesus! God I'm hot. I'm close.'

I wiggle down and tongue her again, this time from behind, licking up and down from her cunt, which is dribbling like a broken tap, to her arsehole which I lick with long deep strokes. She flips around onto her back and locks me on her pussy. I lick till my jaw feels like it's going to go into spasms. My tongue goes numb. Finally I feel her shuddering to a climax. The muscles of her inner thighs relax. For a minute there I thought she was going to cause a cerebral haemorrhage. She sits up.

'Do you want me to pull you off?'

I shake my head. She crosses her arms across her brown, sagging tits.

'You want me to hold you?'

'Yeah . . .'

I lie against her shoulder. I feel very tired.

'Well some things don't change . . .'

'It's the condoms. I hate them.'

'Don't worry about it, baby. Come on, snuggle up to Nancy. You can suck her titty if you like. Just like a baby. That's it, baby.'

Nancy promised us free drinks, so Johnno and I are at the Chauffeur's Club. It's early, before midnight. Only a few strays and losers.

'She knows I can't eat hard eggs, but every morning, she serves the same thing. What is her problem? That's what I don't understand, what is her problem?'

I know her problem. Johnno is the evilest pussyhound I know. He'll cheat on his wife any chance he gets, even if he's not particularly horny. He likes the principle of it. He hasn't touched Susie in years. He says, after four kids, it's like abseiling down the Grand Canyon.

We look around at the available talent. We've never been here before. Johnno screws up his face.

'This is a poofter bar.'

'Waddya mean?' I point out one big burly bloke. Tatts on his arm. 'He's not a poof.'

'Look at the way he's holding that beer. Like a bloody girl. It's fuckin' disgusting.'

I lose interest in the discussion because that's when I see her again. She's wearing the same shabby fake-fur overcoat, clutched to her neck. She looks so fragile, like she's made of porcelain. You could blow her over with a puff. God, she's beautiful. Simultaneously, I well up with tender impulses and stiffen at the dick. I grab Nancy as she passes.

'Who's that girl?'

Nancy looks across the room. She laughs.

'Jesus . . . her! You are such a putz, you know that? It all starts to make sense now.'

Normally I wouldn't let Nancy say that kind of thing to me but tonight I'm mesmerised. My china doll's just taken off her coat, and she's wearing one of those Chinese dresses. High collar, cut-off sleeves. Slit up the side. She's got skinny, long legs in black stockings, sleek as a seal. I wanna run my fingers up that slit. I say to Johnno, 'Don't wait up for me.' He sticks his thumb up in encouragement.

She's sitting by herself at a table for two. I take this as a good sign.

'You remember me?'

'Sorry?'

'From the other night. Crystals?'

She looks puzzled. 'No, I'm sorry.'

I look her dead in the eye. She averts her gaze. She nervously lights a cigarette with an ebony cigarette lighter. Every action is precise, feminine.

'What's your name?'

Her eyes flick up towards me. Reflected light dances over their liquid blackness like flames across an oil slick.

'Lily . . .'

'You want a drink?'

'Brandy, lime and soda'.

Elegant. Everything about her is elegant. I look back on my way to the bar, frightened that she will vanish like a mirage.

'So what do you like to do, Lily?'

'Like?'

'In your spare time? Do you have hobbies?'

She has her chin tucked down, and her shoulders are hunched protectively inwards, as if she's cold. Trying to get her to speak is like trying to get the Pope to fart in public. But I don't hold this against her. She's too beautiful to hold anything against.

'I like to take risks.'

She says this in a husky but girlish voice, and it brings a smile to my face.

'You're a risk taker?'

She nods demurely, then giggles. I know I'm getting places. Her heart is warming to me. I pick up a beer coaster and twirl it around my fingers.

I'm at the bar, ordering us another drink. Nancy is smirking. It makes her yellow-brown, sunspotted face look pinched and thin-lipped. I wonder how I could possibly have found her attractive. I realise that I never have.

'You should avoid that expression, Nancy. You look close enough to a corpse as it is.'

'Having fun, are we, Bill?'

'What's the matter, babe, don't like the competition?'

She laughs in a superior, American way. The condescending bitch. No wonder men go limp around her.

'You are so far up yourself, Nancy. Compared to her, you're like fucking an old sock.'

'She's got a dick, Bill, you idiot.'

I'm lying in bed, breathing heavy. I'm thinking of Serina's mouth on my cock. Thinking of Nancy's tight, thin lips gripping the crown of my dick. Thinking of that girl from the chemist shop who served me Brylcreem, her bucktoothed smile scraping the sides of my shaft. I'm thinking of Elle MacPherson's full, sensuous mouth slurping my pole like a candy stick . . .

Johnno visits. He brings a porno movie—*The Original Gangbang Girl*. Blonde-haired chick called Trixie or Dixie, or something, in this white headband, like she's on her way to Wimbledon. She obsessed with licking cum. Every scene ends with her wearing a pearl necklace. She licks up puddles of cum like a kitten at a saucer. All done with a wide happy smile.

'Look at that smile. You couldn't act that smile. If she was acting that smile, I'd give her an Academy Award.'

'Of course she's acting. She's a junkie. She's probably stoned out of her brain.'

Johnno scowls.

'Your problem, Bill, is you have to think the worst of people. Why can't a girl just like the taste of cum?'

We're at a group cum shot and I can't deny it, Trixie is something else. She's surrounded by a sea of gigantic penises. Some big, some bigger, one blue-veined monstrosity bent almost at right angles. All red and angry, ready to explode. I glance at Johnno, swigging on his beer.

'Hey Johnno, have you ever . . .'

'No.'

'Not even . . .'

'No.'

'What are you doing here?' Nancy sneers at me, as she empties an ashtray. 'I thought you'd be ashamed after what you did to that poor girl.'

'It was a bloke.'

'Whatever. You should still be ashamed. She's smaller than you.'

'Since when did you finish your social work degree?'

'Is that the best you can say?'

I shrug, look down at my beer. I order another one. I think that Nancy's still staring at me, but then I realise she's looking right through me. She's staring at a picture on the wall. A couple of brown-skinned chicks in grass skirts waving their wrists around. Hawaii. I wonder what she's thinking but I don't think to ask.

By the time Lily gets there, I'm as pissed as a urinal. She pokes her head in again, like a turtle coming out of its shell, clutching the coat around her throat. She starts when she sees me, her ghostly face goes whiter. She looks like she's going to walk away, but then stops herself. Hauling herself erect, she strides into the club, straight past me as if I wasn't there.

She takes her coat off. She's in another Chinese dress,

this time in brilliant emerald-green. She looks like a sliver of jade. Softly glowing. Flawless.

I approach her.

'I want to apologise.'

She doesn't look at me.

'I'm not a poof, that's all.'

She lights a cigarette, turns up those hooded black eyes. That impenetrable blackness. An invitation to unspeakable depths. Like an open door. I catch a waft of jasmine oil. I try to make conversation.

'I don't like to hit women.'

She blows smoke in my direction. I find myself fascinated by her lips. Asians have a different texture to their lips. They're more pliant. Moist.

'Can I buy you a drink?'

'I'm meeting a friend.'

'Come on, just one drink.'

'No.'

I watch her all night, talking to this guy in a suit, maybe fifty years old, with dyed blond and blow-waved hair. The kind of man who wears too much cologne. She is different with him. She touches his arm a lot, and laughs loud—maybe too loud. Like the laugh you make when you want to notify everyone in the immediate vicinity about how much fun you're having. She keeps whispering close to his ear. One time he looks over at me, then she laughs again, defiantly.

I don't do anything. I should walk out. I should go over and smack the poofter in the head. But I don't. I sit. I beg Nancy for another beer.

At dawn, I stumble down the stairs and fall over something or someone. I look up and see the sky's greyness and the first hint of rosy light. Then I see her angel face. I smile, glad to see her. Glad that she's followed me. Maybe she's changed her mind and wants that drink with me after all. I try to get up but instead I pass out.

When I wake, I am in Nancy's apartment, on the floor. Nancy is working out to a Cher exercise tape. She is doing the splits in grey lycra shorts with this one-piece singlet thingy that goes right up the crack of her arse.

'What am I doing here?'

'What else? I found you in the gutter.'

I wonder if maybe it was Lily who told her I was there. I imagine Lily going back up the stairs to the Chauffeur's Club, the worried look on her face. Her concern touches me. Then I run to the toilet, fast as I can, to heave out my guts.

'Don't lose a kidney on me.' Nancy strips off the lycra thingy and jumps in the shower. I can smell her sweat as she passes. It's not nice. She smells like a six-month-old fridge. Across her belly runs a large appendix scar, a white streak across an acre of brown. Her arse wobbles like a jellyfish as she turns under the water. I taste a pill of bitterness burst at the back of my throat. Then my mouth fills with vomit.

'Why do you keep coming here, Bill?'

'I can't afford to drink anywhere else.'

Nancy is stroppy. She says the manager has started to notice all the free drinks. I give her one of those puppy dog looks I know she can't resist. She shakes her head and pours me another beer.

Johnno refuses to drink here because of all the poofters, but I don't see it that way. There are queer dogs, for sure, but they aren't interested in each other. They're here for the 'ladies', most of whom are more lady like than the real thing. Even the tragic ones with bent noses, an inch of powder caked over acne pocks and five o'clock shadows still have impeccable manners.

I sit drinking, waiting, drinking, waiting. I don't even know what I'm waiting for, but the more I drink the more I feel a sense of purpose. Every time someone comes in, I look up from my drink, expectantly. I don't even know what I'd do if she came in. I decide that I wouldn't hit her again. Ever. Nor would I propose marriage. I don't know what's happening to me. I have another drink and stop caring.

Shit-faced, I notice across the bar that this guy is staring at me. He's got the beginnings of a pot belly, balding. Stocky kind of guy. The way he's eyeing me, I reckon this ugly cunt is trying to pick me up. He gives me the once over. Sick pervert! Not a chance, mate, not a chance. Then I laugh. Out loud. It's a mirror, you stupid fuck. You're looking in a fucking mirror.

My nose is bleeding, but I gave as good as I got. I don't remember exactly who I hit or why. Maybe they hit me. I take a hankie out of my pocket and watch, from the corner of my eye, the white cotton soak up the blood. On the streets, people are veering away from me. For some reason, I feel elated. Like I've taken a freezing cold shower. All my nerve endings tingle. My head is crystal clear.

I'm walking down William Street, past the hookers in their skin-tight, revealing thingies. A fat one asks me if I want her. I tell her I'd rather wrap my dick around a rancid chunk of blubber. Her reply is most unladylike. It's still only 1 a.m., and I'm ravenous. I stop for a bite at a Chinese takeaway.

It's a cheap, greasy place full of junkies and losers. Two skin-and-bone punks are slumped over a table. Then there's a middle-aged couple. Don't know what they're doing here, probably tourists. Two Maori trannies are shovelling sweet and sour pork into their mouths ravenously. A skinny little Chinese waiter is scuttling between the tables. Even though the place is nearly empty, he seems to be running, scuffling on tartan slippers, the kind you buy at K-mart. He's all hunched over, protecting his chest, as if he's cold. He's got one of those oily faces, his hair lank and flopping over his eyes. I can tell that he's older than he looks.

He puts a glass of water on my table then asks me what I want. I look up, and something about the blackness of his eyes is familiar. And the smell. Jasmine oil. He recognises me the same moment. I can tell, he looks like a rabbit staring into approaching headlights. He hides behind the fringe, hoping for camouflage.

'You're Lily.'

'I'm sorry, my name is Chris.'

'I know who you are.'

'Can I take your order?'

'I love you, Lily.'

This stops him. He looks around. There's an impossibly old Chinese woman watching us. She's got a face like a shrunken head.

'My name is Chris, sir.'

I can't help myself. I grab the glass of water and throw it in his face. The other patrons look at me, startled. The tourists are pleased. They like an incident. Outside, I am furious with myself. I said I wouldn't do that, didn't I? Now what's she gonna think of me? I try to salve my conscience. At least I held onto the glass.

He doesn't finish work until 4 a.m., but I'm there waiting for him. I grab him by the arm as he shuffles past the alley in his sloppy joe and loose pants. He stinks of fried oil and burnt pineapple. His arm is limp, there's no resistance.

'Lily.'

He doesn't say anything.

We go to his place. It's a shabby one-room flat. A mattress on the floor. On the walls, torn up, old posters of Cantonese pop stars. Handsome young men beaming through star filters.

'Get changed.'

He goes into the bathroom. I flop down on the mattress, the sheets are filthy. It surprises me. I always imagine Lily having impeccable hygiene. Beside the bed are a stack of well thumbed magazines. *Vogue, Elle, Women's Weekly*. I spread my arms, feeling surprisingly at home. And tired, like I could sleep forever. I think I must have fallen asleep, I'm startled by the sound of the bathroom door opening.

She emerges from a cloud of steam like a ghost woman from a kung fu movie. A chiffon negligee clings seductively to her sinuous curves. She turns out the overhead lights, so all I see is the silhouette of her from the bathroom light. The stick-like shape of her body, seen through the gown, wobbles precariously as she shuffles towards me in tiny, slippered feet. She sinks to her knees and in the half light I can make out her face, alabaster white, shiny like the moon. There's a strong smell of whisky on her breath, and the line of her lipstick is crooked, but the rest of her is unmistakable. Lovely. Female. Sort of.

She sticks her fingers in my mouth. I feel them forcing something in. A pill. She brings a glass of scotch to my lips. I swallow.

'God, you're good. You're so fucking good. You're so fucking good. God, take it baby, take it baby. Suck it, yeah.'

I feel myself cumming. With both hands I hold her head

in place, keeping her still, pumping my cum down her throat. I feel brilliant. Alive. She doesn't struggle, she swallows. I look into her black, imploring eyes. I long to know what is in those unknowable eyes.

Instead of going down, my cock stays hard like it's charged with electricity. I flip her onto her belly, pull her up on all fours. She half struggles but gives up. She lets me stick it up her arse. There's an initial resistance, a spongy elastic tightness as I probe the hole. Then she opens like a flower in fast motion. I enter in one long, brutal plunge. My cock skewers her arsehole, right to the balls.

I fuck her for all I'm worth, pumping like a steam engine. I reach around and feel for her non-existent tits. The flat, bony ribs are spatchcock-thin, but even this absence is thrilling. I pinch her nipples hard, trying to get a sound out of her, a moan, a cry, anything. My hand slides further down and I touch it. A small, stiff knob, jutting out of her, the texture of velvet. Her cock. I wrap my hand around it and wank. It could be an extension of mine. It's like fucking and jerking off at the same time. It drives me crazy.

She makes occasional, infuriating peeping sounds like a small bird crying for its mother. I wank harder, wanting to tear it right off. I'm soaking with moisture, feeling my love buried in her, wanting to go further, to fill her to the throat, bury myself in her, excavate her, ruin her. I want her to feel what I'm feeling. I want to give her everything. My body feels like it's about to burst into flames. Every part of me burns. I cum again, hot molten lava pouring into her, my fire becoming her fire.

Afterwards, I lay on top of her, gasping for breath. She has flattened against the mattress, motionless, paper-thin, her breath soft. I pull my cock out. There is a glob of shit on the head. I wipe the muck off with the sheet. Surprisingly,

I feel no disgust. In fact, in the half light, the skinny paleness of her skin is unspeakably alluring. I run my fingers along her knobbly backbone. I feel an irresistible urge to kiss her. To hold her close to me and feel the fluttering beat of her heart against my chest.

She turns her head towards me. Her mascara is smeared, the makeup almost wiped from her face. She whispers, in a croaky voice, 'Get out . . .'

I look at her dumbly.

'I said get out.'

I still do not move.

She pulls the wig off, wiping the tears from her eyes, her voice becoming more high-pitched and hysterical. For the first time, she sounds like a woman.

'Leave me alone! Get out! Get out! Get out!'

I don't even have time to button my shirt. When I reach William Street I start to run. The pill is pounding like tom tom drums through my head but it doesn't slow me. I stumble into an old derro, knocking him over, banging my knee against a rubbish bin. I feel an excruciating pain, like something inside is torn, but I don't care. I keep running.

'Hold me, baby, please hold me.'

It takes an hour of persuading, but eventually Serina unlatches the door. Elise is out.

Words pour out of me. I tell her how much I love her, how I'll never do anything bad again, how I don't know how to live without her. I'll spend my whole life down on my knees, worshipping her. Just as long as she comes back to me. Eventually she weakens. The door opens.

'Bill . . .'

'Don't say anything, baby. Don't say anything.'

She doesn't.

THE STAND-IN

BELINDA CHAYKO

'It' (the article, Exhibit G1, the object), when it finally made an appearance in the overly stuffy courtroom, inspired some of the ladies to faint. There was a brief ruckus, much fanning of faces and fetching of tumblers of water, and during this the object was withdrawn. A moment of infamy for the most sordid detail in an already sensational case, 'It' was never mentioned again, although the case ran for several more weeks.

I confess.

I have more than a passing interest in objects of this kind. One could call me a collector, I suppose, though I'm hardly likely to be seen perusing the catalogue at Sotheby's. Back lanes are my territory and the darker, the more lurid, the better. Even then, I find the dealing not nearly furtive enough for my satisfaction at times. I can't stand those places like supermarkets, everything well lit and laid out in shiny rows and the threat of an assistant exhorting me to, 'Have a Nice Day!' after I have just purchased the cruelest of simulacra. An 'object' is not a can of beans, and should not be treated as such. There is no breathlessness in a can of beans, no threat to one's inner being, no implicit crime. (For every 'object' is a weapon of murder, if you'll forgive me for becoming overly metaphorical. And literal—by God, if I donged you over the head with one or two of the more ornamental in my collection you'd be crossing the Styx in no time).

No, I like a seedy but glamorous exchange. Something in *noir*. No eye contact, no words, a well-wrapped parcel exchanged for a discreet envelope containing several untraceable bills. Which is why I now prefer my dealings in foreign countries. After all, it is not the possession of the object that's important, but the acquisition. No one really wants to *fuck* a whore, they just want to *buy* her.

'It' was different.

When I learned of its existence I desperately wanted to have it. I was driven by a need to possess, to know it was mine. Perhaps it was the weight of its history. The case was such a famous one, it feels like something turned on it, there was a shift in thinking, a moral gap opened up. It was the moment in history that allowed someone like me to be born—a public perversion. 'It' was my father and my mother.

(I see you stifling a yawn, bored with my more intricate musings. Let's strike that from the record then. All is forgotten. For the sake of the superficial, and the stupid— that includes you, with your hand still politely covering your mouth—on with the story!)

The truth, the whole truth, and nothing but the truth.

In October 1921, Eugenia F.—the infamous Man– Woman—was convicted of the murder of her first wife, Annie B. The wife had been struck heavily on the head and then set alight, though it was never established whether she was still alive when she began to burn. It was alleged during the trial that Eugenia had murdered Annie when the latter discovered the true identity of her 'husband'. Eugenia, who ran away to sea at the age of fifteen, had lived since then as a man, taking on various aliases, including one 'Harry Crawford'. She had deceived her wife (and several other women, it was alleged) through the use of this particular 'object'. (A ludicrous notion to me, but I hear they only did it in the dark in those days, and it was not uncommon for a woman to never touch a man during love-making except around the head and shoulders. The head, I always thought, had little to do with the matter, but there you go.)

When Eugenia was arrested, she was happily deceiving another wife, by the name of Lizzie, who, according to the transcripts, was deliriously in love with her 'man' and not a whit the wiser when the cops carted Eugenia off. Much was made in court of the search for the 'object', which turned up in a suitcase under the bed (snuggled next to a partly-loaded revolver, a nice touch I thought). It was tendered as Exhibit G1, had the brief appearance I mentioned earlier but otherwise was never described. A psychiatrist's report later mentioned 'a miserable thing, of dirty rags covered with gauze and capped with rubber' and there were other rumours about a table leg, but nothing more specific.

My appetite was moistened. You can see why, can't you? The romance of it, the dirty, filthy, vicious *Mills & Boon*. I can just see the moon on the water, hear the chink of champagne glasses, see the lights go down in the bedroom. Ah, sweet mystery of life . . .

(No, really, do you understand why this thing came to obsess me? And it did, it did. Can you see how the world seemed to lose meaning without it?

Can you?

No? Fine. Leave it. Leave it be.)

This is how one of the most tedious periods of my life began. Traipsing all over the city, going to courthouses, police stations, libraries, for God's sake! Groaning through miles of tedious transcripts, full of 'therefores' and 'if it pleases' and the most despicable forelock tugging, lightened only by the occasional gruesome description of the burned and decaying body of Annie B. (An interesting note: the time of death can be roughly estimated by the size of the maggots chewing on the corpse. The bigger the little beggars, the longer the body has been cold. Useful.)

Cut to the chase: I've tracked 'It' down, to the Police Museum in the middle of the city. 'It' has become Article 35 of the museum's collection and I'm tickled pink by this. The thought of all those school excursions—lines of little angels with falling-down socks and sleepy afternoon faces—all those harried mothers trying to give themselves a break by taking their cherubs to the modern-day equivalent of the chamber of horrors, only to be confronted with a thousand questions about an inexplicable object. The facts of life are hard enough to get across without tying tongues, but the facts of pure pleasure, of a moment devoid of any continuum, of *la petite morte*, *la mort*, *la mort* . . . ah, to be a fly on the wall.

So. I'm driving through the city, one hand on the wheel and the other on myself, foreshadowing the moment of bliss when 'It' would be mine. I had no intention of ever using the object, this must be said. Apart from its obvious fragility (and quite possibly, given the psychiatrist's earlier report, its repulsiveness) I had, already, far too much respect for it. Most in my collection are not fit for use—they are far too ornate, too uncomfortably bejewelled or bevelled around the edges, or just too big, being only symbols after all (and over-inflated ones at that, scarecrow cocks). I did try once, with a quite massive example from southern India and a pretty young thing I'd lured away from a rather petulant boy, much to his surprise, but that's another story.

(Don't think I can't see your revulsion, your reeling back just a little. As you know already, I don't give a toss for your opinion of me, though it has crossed my mind that even you might provide an opportune opening for a little rough play.

But let me plead my case. I am, in the worst possible way, disembodied. Everything I know, everything I do, is framed by this loss, this 'not to be'. All I am trying to do is bridge the gap between me and you and in my case the only means possible are artificial. So don't get on your high horse with me, because *I* know how enamoured *you* are of the fake—in almost all aspects of your life.)

So. I am driving through the city, one hand on the wheel and the other on myself. I pull up in front of the Police Museum (no delays in trying to find a park). My heart is beating a little rapidly, my palms are wet. I try to look nonchalant as I cross the steps. What is a 'normal' speed for walking?, I think, sure I must be moving conspicuously fast. But I am heading in the right direction, the years unrolling beside me—the 70s, the 60s, the 50s. I start to breathe hard and shallow and I can feel an electric sensation starting somewhere in my guts. I turn a corner and run smack bang into the 1920s and have to steady myself.

I move slowly along the glass cabinet, past the guns of various dispositions, the evil knives, the photographic evidence of humanity. Article 38: a switchblade of some elegance which fatally widened the smile of a two-bit hustler. Article 37: removed for repairs, leaving the ghostly trace of a tomahawk. Article 36 (don't you jump ahead now): a scrap of blood-stained cloth, once a cap, which was on the head of Johnnie 'The Jew' Lipnik when it was blown from his body in a dispute over money. Or sex.

I stop. I hold on to the edge of the cabinet, incriminating myself with greasy fingerprints, sucking in my breath then letting it out very, very slowly.

Article 35. Is gone.

Pause. My eyes cloud over as I stand there gripping the

empty cabinet—long enough for one big, hot tear to squeeze out and slide in smooth slow-motion down my cheek, then hang off my chin for a suspended moment before dropping, landing with a splash on my shoe. Exhibit A: one tear-stained canvas sneaker, evidence of a singular folly which ends in a broken heart.

When I can see again I read the small, typed index card explaining the absence of my beloved. Article 35, it said, had disappeared in the relocation of the museum from its former premises some three years earlier. A full and thorough search had been made for the object, which the card declined to describe, but it was never recovered. The card apologised for any inconvenience this may have caused the visitor to the museum. Bitterly inconvenienced, I leave.

I got over it, as one always does, although this one took much more time, and many more foreign diversions, than usual. When I look on it now I wonder what drove me to those lengths, whatever inspired that passion. It looks, from this distance, faintly ridiculous. Though there are times, if woken suddenly in the middle of the night, that I get a feeling of panic somehow connected with this object's nagging absence.

That's the end of the story. I don't expect you to agree, *vis a vis* satisfying resolutions, so in order to round things off I present a proxy for the object. A poor stand-in, as far as I'm concerned, but there seems to be an overwhelming thirst for the sentimental out there that I have never comprehended.

So here it is. Article 34 of the Police Museum, a scrap of a letter sent to Eugenia in jail from her adoring second wife Lizzie after he/she was sentenced to death (did I forget to mention that?). Postmarked November 23rd, 1921. Whether Eugenia ever received it will never be known.

242

My husband,

I have heard what people are saying but do not believe a word. You will always be my darling Harry, my rough little man. So don't you feel bad at all about these things. If there were lies between us, they belonged to us both. I do not know how you can love and not be a liar, they go hand in hand to me. So don't you feel bad about it.

You just remember that I love you. I loved you from the moment you were born, I love you now and will love you forever after.

Your wife, Elizabeth.

SUPERCOLLIDER

CHAD TAYLOR

Carrie Factor waitressed nights. She worked late shifts and spent the early hours of the morning alone in the restaurant, cashing up. Once, the phone rang and she answered and it was some old guy asking what she was wearing. She nestled the receiver in the crook of her shoulder and continued pressing bank notes flat as she told him: I'm wearing my black Mary Janes and black pantyhose and a black skirt and a black bra and a white shirt and a green and blue striped tie. The old guy sounded especially excited when she mentioned the tie. Why are you wearing those clothes, he wanted to know. Because this is a restaurant, she said, and I'm a waitress. He thanked her very much and apologised, because really he was after a domestic number.

After closing the till Carrie would lock up the restaurant and catch a taxi eight blocks to the premises of one Louis Cloud, whom she called Lou and fucked on a regular basis. Carrie and Louis first met at the restaurant. He had booked a table for one and dined slowly and alone. When they were the only people left he paid with cash and offered to escort her to the taxi stand.

They were walking a polite distance apart when, approaching the TV rental store, he reached out and clasped her arm. My favourite window, he said, directing her gaze to the stack of display monitors flickering behind the glass.

Then he snapped his fingers and the television screens began to flash off and on. They switched channels and jumped to full volume, screamed alternate sound bites and hissed and glared. Carrie giggled. Louis grinned and showed her his palm. Learning remote, he explained, returning the device to his pocket. And they carried on walking, their stride leisurely, his apartment nearby.

On the way upstairs she put her arms through his, the old giggly schoolgirl trick. He opened the door to rooms empty of the usual things. No photographs of family or girlfriends, no hallway mountain bike. There was a large European-brand television. And some scotch, to which she said yes.

Carrie sat slightly forward on the red leather sofa, rolling the glass in her palms and looking impressed by practically everything he told her. He'd become slightly nervous, flashing around paraphilia and anhedonicism and prototypical kleptomania like a Dunhill lighter. Gradually, buoyed by her expressions and gentle silences—as elegant as any jargonese—he settled on discussing the more basic parts of his study: new drugs, hopeless cases, non-scientific techniques. When she unbuckled her shoes and raised her stockinged knees beneath her chin, he stopped talking for a minute and stared over her shoulder. What's wrong, she asked. Your drink, he said, taking her glass. And also your shoes, he added in a quiet voice. I'd like you to put them back on. If you don't mind.

She said she didn't mind that at all.

Now, after the restaurant, she returned to his place more often than she went to hers, a three-bedroom flat that had yellowed with boredom and disuse until it consisted only of a bad couch and a forgotten pot of vanilla yoghurt at the back of the refrigerator. Whereas Louis' apartment was clean and permanently new in her mind. He owned a bed the size of a large dining table and when she walked in at one in the morning he was always in it.

It was part of the deal that she never, ever took a shower. She clambered onto his body wearing her work clothes, her shoes catching the sheets, and licked his nipples until his cock turned hard, and after or during this he would wake up and turn her over and press her on her stomach. Louis liked tearing the crotch of her hose and taking her through the rent. He liked leaving marks on her skirt and, especially, her white shirt. He liked to pull out of her just in time to make them.

It was petty to inflict it on someone who wanted nothing more than to be filled with something better than frayed thoughts, but he did it to be petty and she withstood it out of respect for pettiness in general.

Their heads were full of questions. They'd met making commonplace declarations in an uncertain tone: I don't know if this will work; this is the first time in ages for me; I'm not looking for commitments; I'm this, I'm that, I'm feeling really really something—the usual culprits. In the beginning conversation was something that kept your brain from admitting that your body was doing all the work. He loved to watch her mouth, and her eyes. Some people undressed you with their eyes and others just stood there naked. She was the standing there type.

Afterwards she would take off her clothes and have a shower. When she came back to the bed he would be deeply asleep, wearing her torn and sodden pantyhose. He liked pulling them up around his legs as he listened to her in the shower, the water drumming against the basin, the metal popping as she shifted her weight between her feet.

In Louis' mind Carrie stood as tall as him, sometimes taller. As well as her underwear he could fit her jeans and most of her dresses. There wasn't any ceremony attached to the wearing of them—he simply picked them up off the floor, put them on, checked in the mirror, and then took them off again. The first time, she tested his cock as he did so: nothing happened. She liked shaving his face baby-smooth with a razor and applying new brands of foundation, to compare them. She painted lipstick on him and licked it off. He rouged her nipples and her pubis while her hands were tied; painted her toenails as she was pinned unmoving to the bed. She confessed to a failed adolescent dance career. He bought her pointe shoes.

Ticking off on his fingers the clichés that inspired him to erection, pointe shoes were the middle finger. Adjacent digits stood for gags blackened with saliva; shaving her cunt; white ankle socks; and her hair, freshly cut.

The hair-cutting thing began in the first month of winter. She'd spent months growing it long. He gagged her with a handkerchief and shortened the right side by an inch. The crisp snip of the blades was loud in her ears. That night few male diners at the restaurant noticed her shortened bob. Every woman did. She felt herself turning hot with embarrassment. She dropped a plate. She stood before the mirror in the staff washroom and worked herself furiously with her fingers, biting her lower lip until it bled.

The thing about cutting hair was that it couldn't be done gradually. If it wasn't a shock, then nothing had been imposed. A week later she turned up for work looking like nothing on earth. A bad punk, a crazy girl, a villager convicted of wartime collaboration.

He'd cut it by first tying her to the bed and securing her neck in a prone position using a curtain cord. Then he knelt with his legs on either side of her chest and took a handful of her deep black fringe and felt beneath the mattress for the scissors, producing them with a flourish. It didn't seem real to her until he made a chop, taking her bangs back to the roots. Quickly, the numbness in her stomach took over. When he was finished he licked away the tears from her face and released her. She lay back and felt the sheets with her outstretched arms and stared at the ceiling in silence, unable to move.

She liked that. She liked having the words removed from her mouth and the obvious wiped from her brain. He counted a good two or three minutes after fucking before she could string an original sentence together. When she did manage to say something it rarely concerned the events of the previous hour—the sweating or the obscenities or the clothes she was left wearing. Changing the subject was an indirect eulogy. It proved there was nothing left to say on the matter of making love.

The remnants of her $90 coiffure lay scattered on the floor. Standing up, he found her locks and off-cuts sticking to his bare feet like straw. He scuffed his way to the kitchen and edged a frozen block of vodka bottle out of the freezer. Back on the bed, he poured her a shot. She needed it.

He smiled as she rubbed the tear-stains with the back of her hand and ran the other through her crooked shock, wondering aloud what it would be like to live in the courts of the Russian czars. They swapped childhood memories of millifori paperweights, coral frozen in a bubble of glass, and failed interrogations thereof using a hammer and a cement garage floor. She twisted her head towards the dresser, her buckled school shoes leaving black marks on the sheets, and pressed him for details about lighter-than-air transport and *Star Trek* movies. He balanced his shot glass against his lips as he put his thumb inside her cunt. She closed her eyes.

He wouldn't release her until she was late for work.

She stood up slowly, rubbing the circulation back into her limbs, and checked herself in the mirror. Bored with her reflection as it stood he rolled onto his back and watched her upside down, his wet cock fat against the gully of his groin and the warm artery she had licked, pressed against with her ear. He counted down the bumps in her spine from her arse to her head, mentally levelling her clean and beautiful shoulders and the ragged crop of her hair. She wasn't taken aback as much as she'd expected. She was a worse sight than she'd made in the staff washroom a few nights before, but then again a lot better.

She walked around the bed collecting the pieces of her uniform. The shirt was crumpled. She spread the creases flat, pressing down her breasts. She straightened her tie and asked to borrow a pair of jeans. He said they were too big and she said that didn't matter. She unhooked the fly buttons and shook them out by the belt straps. Then she stepped into them and tugged them on. She cinched them with his belt, notching it at the last hole, and walked over to the mirror and turned around and around, watching her arse and her crotch, her flat ashen stomach, her small breasts. He watched her from the bed, monitoring her reflection and her face which wondered, Do you think this is a good thing?

Finally she rolled up the cuffs and put on her makeup. Thickly. She bent over and bussed him goodbye. The shape of her lips stayed behind on his throat.

He listened to her footsteps go down the hall and out the door.

Her shoes were the first and last things about her: first thing he noticed, last thing he heard. Once he unbuckled the left Mary Jane and rested it against her cunt. She probed it with her fingers for a while, then invited him to fuck her with it, the kid-lined heel cupping his balls, his cock bowed inside the toe pressed flat against her pubis. She spent weekday afternoons in factory shops purchasing her favourite styles in a larger size. Salesgirls invariably asked who for. My boyfriend, Carrie would say. He wears them when we fuck. Meanwhile Louis waited outside in the car, counting the seconds until she appeared with a shoe box and a hungry look.

He had wondered initially if this was therapy: if, after completing a special number of perverse scenarios, their true selves would surface. Months later, he realised their true selves were in fact awake and hard at work. They had arrived at the same point too easily for it to be a secret or obsession. They weren't titillated by it. There was no giggling or trembling lower lip. Louis and Carrie shared a language, and they had a lot to talk about.

Louis got up and started cleaning the apartment.

When the head waiter saw Carrie's hair he sent her home for the rest of the week. She disobeyed, and went back to Louis' house. She passed the TV rental shop without pause, although the memory of it still danced in her brain, and entered the hall she'd stepped out of thirty minutes before. He was naked and vacuuming the floor, using the long narrow nozzle to get right into the corners. He gave her a puzzled look. She pointed to her hair. He nodded. She said she'd do the dishes.

He was cleaning the bathroom when she entered still wearing the washing-up gloves and took his cock in her hands. She began to squeeze and pump it, marking its progress. Hot water from the wet yellow rubber was turning the dry flakes around his groin back into mucus.

He unbuckled her belt and undid her-his-jeans and tugged them down. She let go of his cock and rolled around and pushed her arse out towards him and he took her on the side of the bath, his teeth clenched, her rubber gloves squeaking as her outstretched fingers slid on the enamelled steel. The only time they'd made love in her house it had also been in the bathroom on a floor the colour of a sidewalk. He remembered pressing her face forward and making her lick the tiles.

As soon as her hair had grown enough for her to slick it down she returned to work. While she spent the last hour of each evening cashing up alone, he dozed at home in her pantyhose and the shoes she'd bought, sleeping on his stomach if his back was too badly marked. Around one, she stepped into his bed, complaining she was bored—not with you, darling—and he put his mind to it. They decided to get out of town for a while. They decided to leave their clothes behind, pretty much. He cocked the hammer on his credit card. They could have driven down but they booked a plane, and they could have dropped in to see several groups of mutual friends, but they kept their arrival quiet. They weren't going away to see people or new places. They were going away to see each other.

But after stepping on to the aircraft and stowing hand luggage in the marked compartments and following the safety procedure and ordering a couple of stiff gins, they gradually realised they weren't feeling themselves at all. Louis wondered who they'd be facing by the time they arrived at the hotel. Carrie spread the in-flight magazine flat across her stomach and stared out the window, waiting for his fingers to slide beneath the pages. It didn't take long. A little girl sitting across the aisle watched the whole thing, slurping on chocolate milk.

The city seemed bigger than they'd expected and the hotel room smaller. Carrie threw her bag on the bed without much effect. I haven't got any clothes, she said, you haven't got any clothes. He fucked her in the clothes she did have. She slept wearing his Y-fronts. He thought she looked better in them than he did. He sat up watching giant ants consume Los Angeles, the television's flickering light picking out the shape of her body beneath the sheet. He ran his finger along the elastic band of her underwear. She didn't stir. He began stroking between her buttocks and she sniffed and bit her lip, waiting.

The morning was cold. He stepped out wearing her torn pantyhose underneath his jeans. She was bare-legged in her skirt.

They started in the men's wear stores, buying her a pair of jeans in his style. They bought three pairs of boxer shorts in her size, with extra stitching around the crotch and a pronounced arse. She bought a narrow business shirt that spared no room for her bust and a pair of sideburn clippers with extra blades. She picked out lipsticks and foundation, perfume and T-shirts. She had her face done in two different department stores. She listened attentively to sales pitches for depilatories and face cream. On the spur of the moment she had her earlobes pierced a second time, wincing at the counter of the corner chemist.

He didn't enjoy buying things directly. The necessary conversation slowed things down. Instead he discussed options in detail with her as they travelled the sidewalks and, once inside, indicated his preference with a nod or a shrug before slipping away to another part of the store. She bought him calf-length lace-up mules and T-bar dance shoes. She chose white ankle socks and bicycle shorts, dog collars and elbow-length gloves. They bought matching oilskin hoods without the accompanying raincoats. She picked out the longest pantyhose and swimsuits, and upholstery ribbon by the metre. He sat in a dance store reading a magazine while she tried on black ballet slippers, her stare fastened on the saleswoman's hands tightening the laces. Louis watched a little girl go up on pointe for her mother. He could have sworn it was the child from the plane. Carrie came up to him clutching her new shoes wrapped in tissue paper and looking as if she was going to cry.

In the hotel room they ordered room service—steak sandwiches and salad and two bottles of good red wine— and settled down to tearing open the packages. Each item in turn was laid out and inspected. Naked and warm from the shower, they tested lacings and each fit, tried walking and breathing, compared the sheen of leather and cords and the smell of shoes unworn. He put her in the boxers, testing the crotch with his hand, and demanded that she piss in them so he could watch the dark shape spread and chug yellow down her legs. She tasted her ballet shoes and then the inside of the mules before cinching him into them, running her finger up the back of his calves. A lizard stomped across the television and splintered Tokyo. Her fingernails tested the lycra around his legs, rasping. She cut the upholstery tape into two-metre strips and tied him to the bed. And later released him so he could bind her. She wore the ballet shoes, newly anointed, and the business shirt. He found a belt in his luggage and tested it against the air, the hide whistling. She bit into the pillow.

They ate and drank. The late night transmission died. Deprived of quality viewing they turned off the lights and opened the curtains. They counted the stars between the hotel awning and the apartment block next door, a black ribbon speckled with white pepper and the blue warmth of the street lights. She lay in her wet boxer shorts, feeling the damp creep into the mattress. He cradled his chin in the evening gloves, the fingers spotted with mucus and semen, his groin raw. Her nipples ached.

I love the stars. She arched her head forward to sip her wine. Looking at them makes me feel small.

I started off doing physics at university, he said. I wanted to do that instead of medicine.

Why didn't you?

The inhumanity of it. He shook his head, his voice thick. You have to do something practical.

You don't believe that.

It's true.

That's your mother talking, I bet. Your parents.

Pssshhhh. He let his breath out slowly. Pssssssshhhhhh.

She strained to form another sentence. Why did you like physics?

The drama. Balancing his wine glass on his chest, he held his hands wide part, opposing forces. Great things happen in moments of collision. One force meets the other, atoms collide. Bang! He clapped his hands. The wine spilled. She laughed. In a cracked voice he told her the story of the Hindenburg at Lakehurst airfield in 1937, how the big airship had circled to land when static electricity ran up the mooring lines and burned it to the earth in thirty seconds flat. Static, he explained, or the spark from a flashbulb. He snapped his fingers. The hydrogen. Just went up.

She rubbed the crotch of her underpants back and forth, up and down. I don't know what I would have done if I hadn't met you.

He turned his head to face her. The moonlight held the silhouette of her face like curled white paper. She had never introduced the subject directly before. Given the circumstances he didn't think she would raise it again, and he found himself trying to think of what to say, how to cup it in his hands without having it burst.

You would have met someone.

She raised her feet until the slippered toes touched the window ledge. I love these shoes.

He felt his cock harden. I know.

I want to sleep in these shoes. She reached across for his groin. These tights feel good. Is it nice wearing them?

Extremely.

Her fingers searched the broken fabric. Do you have to make the hole with your hands?

He smiled. I could use scissors.

I'd like it if you used scissors.

He ran his fingers through her hair. I could use the clippers.

Yes.

He counted her eyebrows. Do you think it's important for girls to have hair?

For good girls, yes.

What about the others?

She was finding it hard to breathe.

Carrie?

I don't think they should have any. She touched the rim of the wine glass to her lower lip. I don't think anyone bad should.

He waited for her to ask.

Could you please get the clippers? she said, finally.

He smiled and kissed her and sat up. His cock was fully hard now, and she rolled over and kissed it and buried her face in him. The glasses tumbled to the floor. She was still buckling on his dance shoes when he came. The semen hit the right side of her face. She caught it with her hand and tasted it and then he lifted her up to kiss her and slid into her again and held on for just long enough.

A breeze washed through the window, gently curling the curtains. She arched back on his cock, testing its firmness every few seconds. He kissed her nipples. And then they fell apart, spread on their backs. He thought about getting up to find the clippers. He was thirsty.

Is there any wine left? Carrie wanted to know.

We finished the bottle, Louis said. We can order more. He wondered where they'd put the phone. Red or white?

I can't decide.

I'll get both.

Not just yet. She found his hand. Stay with me. And then order the wine.

In a minute, then.

I love the stars, she said again. It all looks such a long way away.

Silently they compiled the things they desired. Each dot of light a possibility, the only respite the blackness in between.

Is your cock hard?

It's sore.

What would it take to make it hard again?

Together they lay there, watching the sky.